Also by Holly Webb

Catmagic

Dogmagic

Hamstermagic

Rabbitmagic

HOLLY WEBB

SCHOLASTIC

First published in the UK in 2009 by Scholastic Children's Books
An imprint of Scholastic Ltd
Euston House, 24 Eversholt Street
London, NW1 1DB, UK
Registered office: Westfield Road, Southam, Warwickshire, CV47 0RA
SCHOLASTIC and associated logos are trademarks and/or
registered trademarks of Scholastic Inc.

ISBN 978 1 407 10984 8

A CIP catalogue record for this book is available
from the British Library.

Printed by CPI Bookmarque, Croydon, CR0 4TD.
Papers used by Scholastic Children's Books are made from
wood grown in sustainable forests.

1 3 5 7 9 10 8 6 4 2

www.scholastic.co.uk/zone

For Jon, Tom, Robin and William

1

Lottie walked slowly up the street, her dachshund Sofie held tightly in her arms, and Giles the hamster perched on her shoulder. Her best friend, Ruby, walked next to her, close enough that Lottie could hear her breathing. It was early on Sunday morning.

Lottie laughed to herself, hugging Sofie closer.

"What is it?" Ruby asked. She looked pale, but she seemed fine otherwise, Lottie thought, looking at her carefully. The spell that had been put on Ruby was definitely gone.

"Oh, I was just thinking. . . When Mum sent me to live here, I had no idea what it would be like. I was just angry that she'd dumped me on Uncle Jack. If you'd told me – what, four months ago? – that I'd be living in a shop full of magical animals,

I'd never have believed you." Lottie shook her head wonderingly.

"Do you – do you wish you hadn't?" Ruby asked her slowly.

Lottie looked up sharply. "Of course not!" She felt Sofie's tense muscles shift with relief. Sofie was Lottie's familiar, her spell-companion, and they were learning magic together. But Sofie was never quite sure how much Lottie loved her, whether she would suddenly decide to go back to her mother, and leave Sofie behind here in Netherbridge. "How could I?" Lottie asked. "There's Sofie, and you, and Uncle Jack and Danny. And all the other animals in the shop. I wouldn't ever want to go back to how I was before. When animals didn't talk, and magic was just in fairy tales." Lottie shivered a little, rubbing her cheek against Sofie's velvet ear, and Sofie licked her lovingly. "It would be better if it was just the good bits of fairy tales, though. I'm not so keen on the evil enchantresses like Pandora. If you'd said we'd be going out on a Sunday morning to fight one of those, I'd have thought you were as mad as Pandora is."

Lottie and Ruby looked at each other and grinned. Lottie had just survived doing the most stupid thing she'd ever done. She still didn't know how. She and Sofie had walked willingly into a fight with a crazed witch. They'd had to. Pandora had had Ruby under a spell, stitched into an enchanted drawing, and it was the only way to save her. Lottie wasn't quite sure how they'd got out alive, let alone how they still had control over their own minds. She shook her head slowly. Everything still seemed to work.

They pushed open the door of Grace's Pet Shop, making the bell jangle cheerfully, and Uncle Jack looked round the door that led on to the kitchen, holding a doorstep of peanut butter toast. "Oh, it's you lot. What are you doing up so early on a Sunday, girls? Want some toast?"

"Can we take it upstairs?" Lottie asked. She was going to have to explain where she'd been to Uncle Jack sometime soon, she knew, but she wanted to talk over everything that had happened with the others first.

Uncle Jack sliced huge wodges of bread and slid them under the grill, and a couple of minutes later Lottie carried a teetering pile of hot buttered toast up the stairs to her room.

"You might bang on Danny's door and ask if he wants breakfast," Uncle Jack called after them.

"On second thought, don't worry, he can make his own; he hasn't set fire to the kitchen for a few months now. If anyone needs me I'll be in the workroom, I've got a big order for Fido's Fang Polish." This was Uncle Jack's own brand of dog toothpaste. It was very popular with dogs, because it was liver flavoured, though he carefully didn't specify liver of what, in case it upset people.

Ruby giggled as they shut the bedroom door and curled up on Lottie's bed with the toast. "Your uncle is so funny. Has your cousin really set the kitchen on fire?"

Lottie let Sofie answer – she'd lived with the family a lot longer than Lottie had. Danny hadn't had any major accidents since Lottie had lived there.

Sofie nodded, the toast crusts sticking out of the corners of her mouth. "Mmmpf. Twice. And when he was four, he flooded it as well. He was trying to make his mother a cup of tea in bed. He put the tea bags in the kettle, and then he left the tap running when he took the tea upstairs."

Lottie smiled sadly. Danny's mum had died when he was seven. Lottie missed her own mum, who was living in Paris at the moment, but at least she got to see her every so often, and they could talk on the phone and send emails. She was there in the background. Lottie couldn't imagine not having a mum at all, like Danny. At least Danny had his dad. Lottie couldn't even remember hers. He'd disappeared when she was two, and had never been heard from again. She couldn't help envying that Danny had his father – well, sometimes. Uncle Jack was great, but he was so scatty! He wasn't much help if you had an emergency geography project and needed a papier-mâché volcano yesterday. Lottie had a feeling that Danny's mum was the kind of person who'd always made sure geography projects got done a fortnight in advance. Which partly explained why Danny and Uncle Jack were now both unbelievably disorganized.

Funnily enough, Uncle Jack was very organized when it came to the shop. He never forgot to feed the animals, or clean out their cages. Although of course it helped that they would complain very loudly if he did.

Lottie jumped as her bedroom door opened. Danny lurched round the door, dressed in tracksuit bottoms and an enormous sweater.

"You've got toast," he told Lottie accusingly. "I

could smell it. Gimme some. Pleeease," he added, as Lottie pulled the toast closer to her. "I'm starved. Hi Ruby." He blinked. "What time is it?"

"About nine," Lottie said. "OK, you can have one piece. And you and Sep have to share!" she added, seeing Danny's black rat appear from his sweater pocket, his whiskers quivering in anticipation of toast.

"Is there peanut butter?" Septimus enquired, leaning over to admire the toast.

"No," Lottie told him firmly. Septimus was incredibly lazy, and very persuasive, much like Danny. She knew he was quite capable of sweet-talking her into going downstairs to get it for him, probably accompanied by another five or so pieces of toast.

"What were you doing up this early?" Danny asked, dropping crumbs all over Lottie's duvet.

"Early!" Giles the hamster tutted. "Best part of the day is before dawn." He nibbled his toast crust delicately for such a chubby creature, filling his enormous pouches.

Septimus eyed him with dislike. "Hamsters, dear chap, are nocturnal. You sleep all day, when we are hard at work."

Lottie half-choked. Septimus went to school with

Danny in his blazer pocket, but neither of them did any work at all.

"Lottie fought Pandora," Sofie told him proudly, as she slyly sneaked another slice of toast.

"What?" Danny yelled, almost dropping his second piece, which he was hoping Lottie hadn't noticed. "Are you crazy? You went and did it on your own?"

"You knew I was going to!" Lottie protested. "You were there when I was talking to Ariadne about it."

Ariadne was Uncle Jack's girlfriend, and a witch. She was helping Lottie find and develop her own magic. Lottie had ended up at Ariadne's flat the previous night. After she'd found a photograph of Pandora with her father, she'd needed answers. Uncle Jack wouldn't tell her what had happened to his brother all that time ago, but Lottie had been sure Ariadne would see that she had to know. She couldn't bear being kept in the dark any longer. Did Pandora have something to do with her dad's disappearance? It had been really weird for Lottie, finding out about her magical family, especially without her dad there. She'd inherited the magic from him, but she didn't have him to teach her – she'd had no idea at all what had happened to him, until odd things had started to happen recently. Ariadne knew and understood all of this, so Lottie trusted her to tell the truth.

"I wasn't going to let you go off, not without someone there for backup," Danny muttered. "I can't believe you just went off and faced her, while I was asleep!"

Lottie wasn't sure if he was cross because she'd done something dangerous, or because he'd missed an adventure, or both.

"She had me!" Sofie said in an indignant growl.

"Hamsters are always proud to be of service," Giles put in.

"And you had me too. . ." Ruby added. "Well, I suppose I wasn't much use." She smiled at Lottie, then she shook her head. "I still can't believe Pandora put me under a spell. It's just – horrible."

"*You* were horrible," Sofie told her sternly. "You were very unkind to Lottie."

Ruby looked hurt. "I'm sorry," she muttered.

"Sofie! It wasn't Ruby's fault!" Lottie put an arm round Ruby's shoulders. "I should be saying sorry to you. None of this would have happened if you hadn't been my friend. Pandora was using you to get to me, that's the kind of person she is."

"Stop wittering," Danny demanded. "What

happened? I mean, you must have won. Unless you're bewitched now – are you?" He stared suspiciously at Lottie, glaring into her eyes, until she grabbed the last bit of toast and shoved into his mouth.

"Shut up, of course we're not." Lottie looked down at her hands. "I don't honestly know what happened. How it ended, I mean, how we survived," she admitted. "It was really weird. . . I . . . I think I saw my dad." She looked up at Danny almost shyly, not sure what he was going to think of her. She wasn't prepared for the expression of pure hurt that flashed across his face, but the moment she saw it she would have given anything to take back what she'd just said.

Danny's voice was slightly flat, but that was the only sign that she'd upset him. "I don't get it. A ghost, you mean?"

"No!" Lottie wasn't sure how she knew that her dad was alive after all, but she did. She didn't look at Danny. There wasn't an easy way to tell him. Having lost her dad, like he'd lost his mum, had always bonded them together, even though they never spoke about it. "No. I think he was real. I'm sure he was." She sighed. "But he was a unicorn." She waited for Danny to snigger. Even

Ruby had thought she was being a bit mad when she'd told her.

Danny leaned back against the wall. "OK. Tell me the whole thing."

Lottie settled her shoulders against the wall next to him and closed her eyes, remembering. "It was awful. Pandora got inside me somehow, and said she could squeeze my heart so it would stop beating—"

"She couldn't do that!" Danny scoffed. Then he looked doubtfully at Sofie. "Could she?"

Sofie shrugged. "I do not know. Perhaps. But she was not trying to. She was just scaring Lottie. And it worked."

"She was scary! I can't help it!" Lottie complained. "She terrifies me. Anyway, Sofie told me she was just pretending, and I snapped out of it, and that made Pandora so cross that she left herself open, and we slipped into her mind."

"Wow!" Ruby gasped. "You didn't tell me that! How did you do it? What was it like?"

Sitting either side of her on the bed, the other two felt Lottie shake slightly. It frightened her even to remember. "Awful. She was so cold, like there wasn't much person left inside her any more. She was frozen."

"We did not stay for long." Sofie laughed, a grim, grunting little chuckle.

"She threw us out, and that was – it was – there was nothing. Only black. I didn't know who I was, even." Lottie smiled gratefully at Giles, who was leaning against her pillow with his paws folded happily across his stomach. "Giles saved us."

"My paw is still not better," Sofie mourned. "I do not think you needed to bite me quite so hard."

"Sofie, dear old thing, you were both unconscious," Giles explained. "I had no choice. I am not by nature a creature of violence –" everyone spluttered slightly, as Giles was a particularly warlike hamster – "but it was necessary in this instance. You woke up, and you woke Lottie up."

"Then what happened?" Ruby asked anxiously.

Lottie frowned, and bit her lip. "Then – I did something stupid. I let her make me angry. She told me she had killed my dad – or she'd sent him to die, anyway. But as soon as I got angry, I was trapped. There was a fire. I mean, I know it was all in my head, but it seemed so real!"

Danny shook his head. "Elementary mistake," he said, in a disapproving, older-brotherly voice.

Lottie glared at him. "I'd like to see you taking it

11

and not getting angry, Mr I'm-going-to-glamour-myself-until-I-fall-off-a-skateboard!"

Danny shrugged, but didn't argue. When he'd started secondary school, he'd tried to use his own magic to make himself popular, but it hadn't worked very well. "Go on then. When did the unicorn come in?"

"About then," Lottie said slowly, remembering. "I called for help. Like I did that time before, when Pandora was in my mind when I was asleep. The unicorn came that time too, and chased her away."

Danny nodded. "Yeah, Dad said about that. He thought you just imagined it. You didn't say it was your dad then, though, did you?"

Lottie blinked. "No. . . I didn't realize. Come on, Danny, it was a unicorn! And everyone's always told me my dad was dead! What was I supposed to think?"

"So how do you know it was him this time? Did he say so?" Danny's face was painfully eager.

"No. He just said he'd always come if I called him, I only had to ask. But Pandora recognized him; she yelled, 'You!' She screamed it out, like it was being . . . torn out of her heart. . ." Lottie took a deep breath. "It was then I realized who he was.

Pandora sort of stepped back, and she was staring at us both. I don't think she could have hurt us; it was like she was in shock. Then I don't know what happened, but the unicorn was gone, and so was Pandora."

"But how? How could you tell it was him?" Danny demanded again, and Lottie looked at him helplessly.

"I'm so sorry," she whispered. "I just could."

"I don't understand," Ruby murmured. "I mean, I don't understand any of it really, but what I don't get is why your dad turning up shocked Pandora so much. She'd tried to kill him, I guess. Was that it? She thought he was dead, and he wasn't?"

Lottie laughed, but it wasn't a happy laugh. She sounded bitter. "Sorry, Ruby, I forgot you didn't hear about that. I found it all out while you were under that spell. Pandora was my dad's old girlfriend."

"What?" Ruby squeaked. "You're kidding!"

"Nope. Ariadne told me. They went out for years. Before he met my mum. But he broke it off with her, because she was trying to control him. She tried to get between him and Uncle Jack – she was jealous, I think. Uncle Jack and my dad were

13

really close, and she didn't want anyone to have a piece of my dad but her."

"I can believe that," Ruby muttered. "She's mad, isn't she, totally off the charts?"

"Beyond mad," Lottie agreed. "I thought she really hated me – I still think she does, actually. And she sent my dad off to get killed all those years ago; she laughed about it! She was gloating. But she said I looked like my dad, and maybe when he was there too, she remembered how close they used to be." She shrugged tiredly. "I don't really understand. But I think – I think Pandora wanted to use me."

"What for?" Ruby asked plaintively. Lottie was working it all out as she went, now she had the time to think, and it wasn't the easiest thing to follow.

"She wanted to control me. I mean, think about it. If she could get at your dad, Danny, he's the very first person who took my dad away from her. Uncle Jack was closer to my dad than she was, that's what broke them up. She's been desperate to get back at the whole Grace family ever since." Lottie stared at Danny and Ruby, her face serious. "If she could enslave me, and use me to torture all of you somehow – use

14

Tom's own daughter – it's the ultimate revenge, isn't it?"

Danny gazed back at her. "We were lucky your dad turned up when he did," he said quietly. "Even if he was wearing hooves."

Ruby coughed apologetically. "I'm really sorry to keep asking stupid questions, and it's probably obvious, but – *why* is he a unicorn?"

Lottie looked hopefully at Danny, but he shook his head. "Haven't a clue."

Sofie sighed irritably. "I keep telling you all! He is *not* a unicorn! He's a dream creature. A vision. He was not really there!"

Lottie's heart suddenly pulsed with fear. "You mean, he isn't real?" she asked painfully, her eyes fixed on Sofie. "I just imagined it? But I was so sure."

Sofie shook her head so hard her ears flapped. "He is real somewhere, Lottie *cherie*, do not be afraid. And the unicorn is part of him somehow. I do not know how he is doing it. I suppose he had to pick a shape to come to you with, and that is what he chose. I wonder. . ."

"What?" the others demanded, after she trailed off in this tantalizing fashion.

"It was just a thought," Sofie mused. "I

wondered if perhaps he has lost his own shape somehow – in his head, at least."

Lottie looked at her worriedly. She supposed that she ought to be grateful that her father was alive at all, considering that an hour or so ago she had been sure he was dead. But someone who had lost their shape sounded scary. *Sofie's just thinking aloud*, she told herself firmly. *She can't be right all the time. Can she?*

"Lottie! Lottie, you aren't listening!" Giles's breathy, squeaky little voice broke through to her at last, and she blinked. "No one is thinking about the important question," he told her sternly.

Lottie frowned. To her, what shape her father was seemed pretty important, but she looked enquiringly at Giles.

The plump hamster leaned in towards them all and hissed, "Where is Pandora now?" Then he sat back, paws folded, and gazed at them triumphantly.

Lottie shook her head. "I don't know," she murmured. "I sort of hoped she'd run away. But – I'm not sure if she's the sort of person who does that."

"Exactly." Giles nodded, his beady little black eyes sparkling. "We need to be in a state of high alert, in case she comes back." He actually rubbed his paws together. Clearly the thought of a possible attack was just what he wanted.

Lottie wished she could be as bloodthirsty, or if not, at least as brave. The idea that Pandora could be back at any time didn't make her feel warlike. It made her want to hide under her duvet and shut out enchantresses, and fathers who had disappeared and then reappeared as mystical animals, and just everything, to be honest. Tears burned at the back of her eyes. Everything was so difficult.

Sofie nuzzled at her arm, nudging Lottie with her velvety black nose. "Do not worry, Lottie. I will not let her harm you, I promise."

The thought of a small, but very determined, dachshund standing up for her against Pandora made Lottie smile, even if it was rather limply. "I'll be all right," she said firmly, stroking Sofie's head. "It's only that sometimes I wish all I had to worry about was homework."

Lottie sighed, but Sofie stared back at her disapprovingly. She refused to allow Lottie self-pity. Sofie regarded wallowing as a waste of good chocolate-eating time. She shook her head at Lottie. "Well, *ma petite*, that would be very boring, do you not think?"

2

Lottie and Ruby headed across the playground, not talking, just silently comfortable with each other. It felt nice to know that they would be walking home together again, Lottie thought to herself, smiling a little. Because of Pandora's spell, Ruby had hardly been talking to her at all. It wasn't that they'd argued, or even grown apart – Ruby had just suddenly seemed to go from being Lottie's best friend to forgetting that she existed. Lottie had spent one journey home from school walking behind her, not even sure that Ruby really knew she was there. She shook her head briskly, trying to get it out of her mind.

Ruby nudged her with her bag. "What are you thinking about?" she asked. "You look worried."

Lottie smiled at her. "Just remembering last week."

Ruby's face fell dramatically. "Lotti-eeee. . ." she wailed. "I've said I'm sorry! I didn't mean to, it was all the spell, honestly it was."

Lottie hugged her. "I know that, dimwit! I was just being glad that we were friends again."

Ruby didn't say anything for a moment. She just stared at the ground. "I didn't miss you," she said slowly. "I'm not sure I actually thought much about anyone. I didn't even realize we weren't friends any more. Everything went blank." She glanced up at Lottie for a second to see if this had shocked her.

Lottie only nodded. "Mmmm. I suppose if Pandora had wiped half your mind away, everything that was left was just concentrating on getting through the day. Not much space left for thinking about stuff." She resisted making a jokey comment about that being pretty normal anyway; Ruby didn't seem to be in the mood. Lottie found it helped, being silly about Pandora. It was a bit too scary to think about her otherwise.

"I think you're right. I can't remember anything about that week – it's like I sleepwalked through it." Ruby shivered. "Do you think I'd have stayed like that for ever, if you hadn't broken the spell?"

Lottie walked on silently for a few steps. "I honestly don't know," she admitted. "But I think maybe. Unless she had to keep thinking about the spell to make it work. What did you do with the drawing?"

"I burned it." Ruby tucked her hands under her arms, as though to stop them shivering. Ruby had found the drawing that Pandora had used to create her spell, folded up very small in her own coat pocket that morning after Lottie had fought Pandora. It was one of Ruby's mother's drawings, and it had been amazingly lifelike. Ruby stared sideways out of the page, half-smiling. Pandora had stolen it from Ruby's house, and when they had found it it had faded strangely, as though Pandora had sucked the life out of it. "Even though I knew you'd broken the spell, I couldn't bear to look at it any more. Mum liked it more than I did anyway; she made my nose look huge." Ruby smiled a little. "She still can't work out where her sketchbook's gone. I guess Pandora just threw it away. And that's the other scary thing, Lottie. Pandora must have been inside my house to steal the sketchbook. What else did she see? That's what worries me. Did she steal something else – or – or even leave something in the house, watching us?"

Lottie shook her head. "I don't think she would have done – she was too focused on getting you to do what she wanted, she didn't need to do anything else. But if you're worried, let Sam and Joe out of their cage one day, when your mum's shut away painting. If Pandora's left some sort of spying spell, I'll bet those two could sniff it out, no problem. It was them that worked out what was wrong with you, you know. They really watch out for you."

Ruby laughed, but she was pink with pleasure. Sam and Joe were her gorgeous blue lizards – they claimed they were a smaller species of dragon, but Lottie wasn't sure if that was just what they wanted to believe.

"They are fab, aren't they. . .?" Ruby murmured happily. "Actually, that reminds me, they've been moaning like anything that their tank isn't warm enough now that the weather's getting colder. I promised I'd look in the pet shop down by the bridge and see if they had anything to help. I've got a horrible feeling it might mean a new tank, which would be Christmas and birthday presents for the next seventeen years. Mum still hasn't got over the shock of how much Sam and Joe cost in the first place."

Ruby's lizards had accidentally ended up in a huge pet shop in a big town not far from Netherbridge, where none of the staff had any idea what they were, or quite where they'd come from. Ruby's mum had agreed to buy her a hamster, but they'd walked out half an hour later with two turquoise-blue dragons instead. Sam and Joe had liked the look of Ruby, and they had enough magical power to have been able to suggest very firmly that she and her mum should take them home.

Now that Lottie had told Ruby all about magic, Sam and Joe talked to her too. She adored them, even if they were nearly as bossy as Sofie.

Ruby looked at Lottie worriedly. "You don't mind, do you? I don't think your uncle's shop has stuff for lizard tanks."

"Don't be silly, of course I don't mind. Uncle Jack mostly does just the animals, and special foods and things. Can I come with you?" Lottie asked interestedly. She'd never been in the other shop. It was a normal pet shop, selling mostly pet food and bedding, that kind of thing. They had a few animals, but nothing very exciting, not that she'd heard about, anyway. It would have felt a bit like betraying Uncle Jack to go and look round a different pet shop. But if Ruby wanted something that her uncle's shop didn't sell. . .

"It's nothing like your uncle's shop," Ruby warned her.

Lottie grinned. "I bet it's quieter."

"Mmm." Ruby nodded. "But now I've seen all the pets at your place, the other one just seems really sad. I feel like all pet shops ought to have pink mice dancing the conga along the shelves."

The pet shop was in a row of little shops: a rather dingy café advertising all-you-can-eat breakfasts served all day, the sort of hardware shop that sells absolutely everything, all tucked away on hundreds and hundreds of tiny shelves, and a shop that sold knitting wool, with a window full of ugly jumpers.

The pet shop's window was so covered with posters for cat foods that would give your cat fresh breath and a glossy coat, new improved dog-training whistles, cuttlefish bones, and *LOST, small white spaniel, answers to the name of Mags*, that Lottie couldn't really see much inside. The door squeaked shrilly as it swung open, and a dank smell of

23

grubby cages rushed out at them, making Lottie grimace.

"Told you," Ruby muttered, and the door clanged shut behind them.

The shop was rather dark and muddled, but not in the nice way that Uncle Jack's shop was. There the walls were covered in cages and piles of things, but everything was clean and fresh-smelling. Lottie thought Uncle Jack must have stretched the space by magic somehow, when he couldn't bear not to have some new sort of animal, because no one would have built a shop with quite so many odd corners and crannies and little strange spaces. The muddle in this shop was dusty and musty and old. The cages didn't look dirty – they were almost all empty anyway – but the underlying smell made Lottie want to sneeze.

No one was sitting behind the counter, so the girls wandered around, poking into piles to see if there was anything to do with warming up lizards in them.

"What are we actually looking for?" Lottie asked, holding a pink fluffy cat coat in dismay. No self-respecting cat would be seen dead in it. "Sort of lizard hot-water bottles?"

"I don't know," Ruby said thoughtfully. "I thought a new heat lamp for their tank – they're like artificial sunlight, you know? But Sam said what he'd really like were hot stones that he could lie on. I don't know if you can even buy those. I've a feeling that the sort of lizard they are might be used to living quite close to volcanoes."

Sam and Joe hadn't told Ruby they were actually dragons yet. Lottie thought they didn't want to upset her. Besides, with all their research into flame production, she might be a bit worried about them living in her bedroom. But now that Ruby knew everything about her uncle's pet shop, and Lottie's own magic, Lottie thought there wasn't much that could shock her. After all, she'd taken the amazing news about Lottie's dad pretty well – and that had taken some believing.

Lottie sighed. She wished she knew what to think about her father. Or what was going to happen now. It had thrown her completely, because she had known he was dead. Her mum had *always* said so. Would Lottie ever see him again? She had a feeling that she would, but when? She really wanted to know, for certain.

"What do you two want?" snapped a grumpy voice, and Lottie jumped and knocked over a stack of chew toys and a plastic Scottie wearing a tartan dog coat. She scooped them up guiltily, while a little old lady with a sour, pinched face glared at them both.

Ruby started to explain what they were looking for, while the old lady alternated between grumbling about how much she hated reptiles and glaring at Lottie.

"We've got nothing like that. Lot of nonsense," she muttered, when Ruby finished her halting description.

Ruby sighed and was just turning to leave, when something in the tottering pile behind the old woman's head caught her eye. "Oh, but look! Reptile sun lamp! You do have one, up there!" she pointed out.

The old woman looked so cross that Lottie wondered if she just hated selling things. Lottie couldn't see how the shop stayed open, if she was this nasty to everyone who came in. Or maybe she just didn't like children.

With much complaining, the old woman fetched a step stool, and started to reach for the lamp. Lottie, having already knocked over one pile, decided the best thing to do was stay out of the way. She retreated back away from the counter to look at a shelf full of mouse bedding, and came face to face to with a rabbit.

Or rather, face to bottom. The rabbit's cage (which looked horribly small for him) was tucked away on a big shelf between the mouse bedding and stones for the bottom of fish tanks. He was facing into one corner, looking at the wall. Lottie immediately got the sense that he wasn't happy. She wasn't sure any creature could be, all squashed up in this gloomy, miserable shop. The only other animals she'd seen were a tank of depressed-looking goldfish, with *Buy One Get One Free* plastered across the front of them. Lottie thought fish were probably dim enough not to mind. But the rabbit was suffering, she could tell.

"Hey," she whispered, and the rabbit twitched a little. But he stayed staring at the wall. "Are you all right?" Lottie wasn't sure if she was expecting the rabbit to answer. Surely they wouldn't have magical creatures in this grim place? Unless it was some awful mix-up, like with Sam and Joe. Lottie felt sorry for even an ordinary pet shut up here. The rabbit peered over his shoulder hopelessly, his eyes dull. He blinked at the sight of Lottie, and his ears wriggled slightly. A faint gleam shone in his eyes, and he put his head on one side thoughtfully.

Then he shuffled round so that he was looking at her properly.

"Do you – like it here?" Lottie asked, waving a hand at the dusty piles of stuff around his cage.

The rabbit gave her an expressive look. *What do you think?* he seemed to be saying.

Lottie nodded. "It's pretty awful, isn't it. . .?" she murmured.

"Don't bother the animals!" the old woman shouted across the shop. "I won't have the likes of you upsetting them. You ought to be ashamed of yourself!"

"Me!" Lottie shot back, whirling round. Living with her snappy, opinionated familiar Sofie, who was a very determined French dachshund, had given her much more confidence to argue with people. Even before she and Sofie had shared their magic and their thoughts, people being mean to animals had been the one thing that could make Lottie see red. She stalked back over to the counter. "I'm not upsetting him! He's miserable, can't you tell? He was just staring at the wall!" She could feel Sofie, back at home, waking up from a nap all excited. Sofie's soft black furriness wrapped round her, telling her to keep going. "He shouldn't be in a tiny little cage like that, anyway."

"You mind your own business!" the old woman snapped.

"Cruelty to animals is everyone's business," Lottie told her. She had no idea where she was going with this. She didn't have enough money to buy the rabbit, and she was sure that the rabbit wasn't actually being badly treated enough that she could report the shop to the RSPCA or anywhere like that. He was just miserable.

"Cruelty! Right. Both of you, out of my shop, this minute. Cheeky little devils, I'll have the police on you!" And the old woman surged round the counter in a rush and hurried them out, squawking and gobbling like an angry, scrawny-necked chicken.

As she bustled them out of the door, Lottie looked back and saw the rabbit sadly turning around to face the wall again. That one glance back decided it.

She was going to get him out of there.

Unfortunately, she had absolutely no idea how.

"Wow," Ruby murmured, as the door squeaked shut again in a determined manner. "She wasn't a witch or anything, was she?"

"No, she was just mean," Lottie said, staring back into the pet shop window, and resisting the urge to make faces. The old lady was still staring at them, and she was holding her telephone with her finger poised meaningfully over the buttons. "I suppose we shouldn't have let her shove us out, but I couldn't see how to stop her. I mean, it is her shop, and she hadn't actually done anything wrong."

"You were right, though," Ruby told her. "The rabbit did look totally depressed."

"Oh, good, I'm glad you thought so too, and I wasn't just being stupid." Lottie looked back through the window. "Come on. Let's go back to our shop. I want to ask Uncle Jack if there's anything we can do."

They set off, walking slowly, and looking back at the dirty windows of the shop every so often. "I hate to leave him there," Lottie muttered. "He looked so hopeless. The way he just turned round to the wall again. I bet he never gets taken out of that cage for a cuddle."

"He wasn't a talking rabbit, was he?" Ruby asked.

Lottie wrinkled her nose, looking quite like a rabbit herself for a moment. "I don't think so. . . But even if he was, with no one around to talk to him, and stuck in that awful place, he might even have forgotten how to. Or just never learned, like Tabitha the cat hadn't. There was something about him. He had such lovely eyes. Really big and soft-looking, almost like he could talk with those."

"We can't leave him there," Ruby said firmly. "I guess we could buy him."

"Have you got any money?" Lottie asked hopefully.

Ruby shook her head. "Sam and Joe are really expensive to feed. I have to buy them locusts, and, um, mice and stuff. . ." She knew how much Lottie loved mice, so she didn't like to mention Sam and Joe's eating habits.

"Urrgh." Lottie shuddered. "I'm really glad Uncle Jack only has small lizards. Imagine our mice watching the lizards having lunch, that would be awful." She sighed. "I haven't any either. And I'm not sure she'd sell the rabbit to us anyway, just out of spite. I suppose we could send Danny."

"Or I could ask my dad, if we explained," Ruby suggested. "He really likes animals; he'd understand. It's just that he's so busy with work, I hardly get to see him."

"Mmm." Lottie thought about Ruby's dad. At least when Ruby saw him he was real. Lottie wondered what her own dad was doing right now.

It was so odd to think that she had seen him at the weekend, just like any other person whose dad didn't live with them all the time.

Lottie still didn't know people that well at the school in Netherbridge, but at her old school, at least a third of the class didn't live with both their mum and dad. Lots of people had half-brothers and -sisters. It had made it easier for Lottie. No one had been very surprised that her dad wasn't around. Quite a few of her friends weren't there for sleepovers and stuff at the weekend because they'd gone to see their dads.

But then, their dads were just living in a flat somewhere a little way away, they weren't lost in the rainforests of the Himalayas chasing unicorns. And when Lottie had seen her dad, he'd actually *been* a unicorn. Somehow. And he hadn't really been there, he was just a vision, or so Sofie said.

"It's not just the rabbit making you miserable, is it? Are you worrying about your dad again?" Ruby asked her gently, touching her arm.

Lottie blinked at her, coming slowly out of the memory, her eyes hot and scratchy with tears. She nodded. It wasn't fair to resent Ruby because she saw her dad every day, even if it wasn't for very long. One tear dripped down Lottie's nose as she thought again how much luckier she was than Danny. His face flashed into her mind, that look of loss when she'd told him what she'd seen. Her dad *was* alive, after all. His mum wasn't going to stage a magical reappearance.

But still, she almost envied Danny, too. At least he was certain what was going on with his family. He'd actually seen his mum buried. He went to visit her grave sometimes, with flowers. And his dad was there with him every day, even if he was a bit ditzy. He was *there*. Not off in another country for work. *One parent missing is understandable*, Lottie thought to herself. *But losing both of them, Lottie, that's just careless.*

"I just wish I knew what's going to happen," Lottie whispered. "If he's coming back or not. Maybe he can't. Will I ever see him properly? I know he's alive, but I still don't ever get to hug him, or have him come to the school for parents' evening, or anything." She stared at Ruby, hating to say it, but desperate to tell someone. "I'm not sure I wouldn't rather he was still dead," she said in a rush. "I can't stand this not knowing. It doesn't make me feel better that he's alive. It just makes me feel sick."

3

When Lottie and Ruby got back to Grace's Pet Shop, Lottie scrubbing her eyes determinedly with a manky-looking tissue she'd found at the bottom of her coat pocket, they couldn't help smiling at the difference from the shop by the bridge. As they pushed open the door, one of the pink mice was standing on the counter, demonstrating to Uncle Jack and Ariadne that he really could balance an acorn on his nose. He froze as the doorbell jingled, and the acorn fell off, very slowly, and plinked across the counter.

"Oh, it's you!" Fred the mouse scolded. "I nearly went white! Could you try *not* to do that sort of thing?"

"Sorry," Lottie told him, grinning. Fred always cheered her up.

"You're late back, girls," Uncle Jack commented.

"Lottie came to help me look for a new sun lamp for Sam and Joe," Ruby explained. "We – er – we went to that other pet shop down by the bridge?" She looked worriedly at Uncle Jack, hoping he wouldn't be annoyed.

Uncle Jack frowned slightly. "What was it like?" he asked. "I haven't been past it recently, but it's always looked a bit grotty to me."

"It was horrible," Lottie told him.

"They had a lamp, but it wasn't as good as the one Sam and Joe have got now," Ruby added.

"Did they have any animals?" Uncle Jack looked anxious. "I hope not; it looks so depressing in there."

Lottie nodded. "Not many. There was a fish tank, but the fish looked OK, but there was a rabbit too, Uncle Jack, and I'm really worried about him."

"A rabbit?" Uncle Jack looked thoughtful. "A white one?"

"No, a sort of soft grey, and really sweet. He had enormous ears, twitchy ones. He hated it in there, you could tell." Lottie's voice shook. The rabbit had made her feel so sad, and so angry at the same time. No one should be allowed to keep an animal in a tiny cage like that.

There was a brisk flurry of clicking sounds, as Sofie galloped down the stairs and skidded into the shop. "Lottie! You're back! If only I'd been with you, I could have bitten that woman for you," she told Lottie sadly. "Why were you so angry with her? I was half asleep, I couldn't tell."

"She was being cruel to a rabbit," Lottie explained, picking Sofie up and hugging her.

"Lottie told her off," Ruby added. "You'd have been proud of her."

Sofie sniffed. "Rabbits are stupid. All they can do is jump out of hats. What is the point of that, hmm?"

Ariadne laughed. "I think humans make them do that, Sofie, because they think it's funny. I don't think rabbits actually *like* hats very much."

"Well then, they should not do it," Sofie said dismissively. "Why are we bothering with this rabbit, Lottie? I am not interested in boring rabbits. They have no conversation."

"I'm not sure this is actually a rabbit that can talk at all," Lottie admitted. "But it's shut up in a mean little cage in a grubby pet shop, Sofie. It was really beautiful, with gorgeous big eyes, like yours, only really sparkly. It was so sad, shut away like that. We have to bother with it."

Sofie blinked at this description, and seemed about to say something. Then she shrugged, which was quite a major operation for such a small dog. Her shrug started with her ears and went all the way to her tail. "Oh well, if you say so," she agreed, in a most uninterested voice.

Lottie was rather shocked. She knew that Sofie was lazy and chocolate-obsessed, but she hadn't thought that she wouldn't care about another animal being badly treated. In fact, only a couple of months before, Sofie had helped her rescue Tabitha, the little brown tabby cat who was now Ariadne's familiar. At the time, they had both thought that Tabitha was just a grubby stray. Who knew what this rabbit could be?

Tabitha sensed that Lottie was thinking about her. Ariadne was sitting on the edge of the shop window, and Tabitha had been dozing in the velvet bag at her side. She woke up with an enormous yawn and stepped delicately out of the bag, blinking.

Fred immediately whisked back up the shelves to the safety of his cage, spitting mouse insults. "You didn't tell me she was here!" he squeaked angrily at Ariadne. "I could have been mortally wounded. Two shocks in one day; my coat will never be the same again."

Tabitha jumped gracefully on to the counter and politely touched noses with Sofie. They tolerated each other, but they would never be friends. She purred at Lottie and Ruby, which made Sofie's whiskers bristle.

"Isn't Shadow with you?" Lottie asked, and Ariadne and Tabitha exchanged a worried glance.

"He was too tired," Ariadne explained. "We left him back at the flat, sleeping."

"Again," Tabitha mewed. "It's all he does these days," she added in a mutter.

Ariadne sighed and stroked her gently. "I know it's boring for you. But he's such an old cat. He needs to rest."

Tabitha jumped back on to Ariadne's lap and rubbed her head lovingly against her mistress's cheek. "I know. I'm only grumpy because I'm worried about him," she murmured. Then she turned round to eye Sofie and Lottie. "You ought to help this rabbit," she told them. "If you hadn't helped me, I would never have found Ariadne. And she would probably have ended up with that frightful Selina as her new familiar."

There was a grumpy hiss from the next room,

where the black cats, Selina and Sarafan, had their pen.

"Another thing to do," Uncle Jack muttered, tying a knot in his handkerchief. "I must find those two an owner; they shouldn't be shut up in that pen all the time, at their age."

"But Uncle Jack," Lottie complained, "their pen is huge! I know they're actually locked in it, and most of the animals aren't, but it's still like a great big cat palace! You should have seen the tiny little cage this rabbit was in."

Uncle Jack looked apologetic. "I know, Lottie. But rabbits are used to being shut up, and cats aren't. They're free-range pets. I only keep Selina and Sarafan shut up because *I can't trust them*!" He said the last bit in a very meaningful voice, and a sniggery little purr answered him from across the shop.

Not only were the two cats extremely greedy and prone to chasing and, if possible, eating anything that moved, they were also master criminals. They were now up to six padlocks on their pen, and the latest one had a combination number. Every time anyone walked past the pen, the cats would ask them seemingly idle questions about birthdays and house numbers, and if the person was foolish enough to answer, they would go into a huddle and start frantically working out possible combinations. Whenever the shop was quiet, one could hear a gentle *click-click-click* of tumblers turning, as the cats delicately manipulated the lock. Lottie happened to know that Uncle Jack had actually set the combination as 1234, because he hated that sort of thing and always forgot numbers. Luckily, Selina and Sarafan were far too devious to believe that anyone would use a code that simple, so they would probably never find it out.

"This rabbit didn't like being shut up, Uncle Jack," Lottie assured him. "He was really miserable. Can't we rescue him somehow?"

"He looked ever so sad," Ruby agreed.

Ariadne and Uncle Jack looked at each other. "Well, I suppose you could try a calling spell," Ariadne suggested.

"Good idea." Uncle Jack nodded happily. "And good practice too."

"How does it work?" Lottie asked eagerly. "I could go and try it now."

"Homework," Horace the parrot grunted warningly from his perch in the window. He had taken it upon himself to educate Lottie, since he'd tested her on her spelling words and discovered she still mixed up *threw* and *through*. He thought she wasn't being taught very well, and kept reciting Latin grammar at her when she wasn't expecting it. He swore it would come in useful one day.

"I promise I'll do my history first," Lottie assured him. "We've got to look up something about Egyptians on the computer, that's all. I can be thinking about the spell while I'm doing that, though, can't I?"

"Computer," Horace growled dismissively. "Lot of nonsense. Can you girls recite all the kings and queens of England? You cannot. Shameful."

"But I know the Egyptians used to pull dead people's brains out of their noses with a special hook," Lottie told him brightly. "That's much more useful."

Horace turned his back on her and ruffled his feathers up irritably. Ruby giggled.

Ariadne sniffed. "Ridiculous idea. Completely pointless thing to do. Anyway. For a calling spell you need to think very carefully about the creature you're calling," she explained. "Especially think about its magical self. Try and call to that. You might find you need a picture to look at, and sometimes fresh herbs can put you in the right mood. You remember the ones we talked about?"

Lottie frowned. "But I'm not sure this rabbit *is* magical. How can I think about its magical self if it doesn't have one?"

"Oh. . ." Ariadne looked blank. "I hadn't thought of that. I usually work with magical animals."

"It might work with an everyday rabbit, if you think hard enough about what made him special," Uncle Jack mused. "You mentioned his ears, and his sparkly eyes. Remember that sort of thing, and call. Sofie can help. I know she didn't see him, but having your familiar with you helps you make your spells stronger."

Lottie looked doubtfully at Sofie, who was staring vaguely out of the window. She didn't seem in the slightest bit interested in making any spells stronger. Not those to do with rabbits, anyway.

"I'd better get home, Mum'll be looking out for me," Ruby said, picking up her school bag. "Meet you by the bridge before school tomorrow, Lottie, OK?"

Lottie waved goodbye to her and looked round to ask Sofie if she wanted to share a banana while they looked up stuff on the computer. But oddly, Sofie had disappeared.

She didn't turn up all evening, and Lottie fretted, getting crosser and crosser. Sofie *knew* she wanted to try the calling spell. Where had she gone? Lottie was actually forced to do some homework in advance, and she was so grumpy she didn't even feel virtuous.

Sofie eventually sneaked through her bedroom door, looking innocent, just as Lottie was about to go and brush her teeth.

"Where have you *been*?" Lottie demanded, her voice squeaking with crossness.

"I was busy," Sofie retorted, stalking across the rug with her nose in the air and scrambling up on to the bed.

"But the spell!" Lottie folded her arms and glared.

"We can do it tomorrow." Sofie's voice was muffled. She was curled into a velvety black doughnut shape, her nose buried under her tail. She wasn't moving.

Lottie huffed in exasperation and went off to the bathroom.

Maybe it was the anger and frustration with Sofie that opened her mind, or maybe it was that Sofie had withdrawn herself a little, leaving the way to Lottie's mind open, but that night, Lottie dreamed.

More than a dream. A vision. A message.

Lottie was thundering across the ground under a starlit sky, her feet thudding. No, her hooves. Lottie had a moment of horrible panic, where her galloping stride caught and stumbled. She was a unicorn now too!

"Don't fall, little one." Someone was galloping beside her. Someone had slowed their breakneck pace to nudge her onwards. Lottie strode out gratefully, matching her pace to the larger creature beside her. Her long mane floated out behind her in the whirlwind of her gallop, and her ivory hooves beat out a strong, confident rhythm. Lottie relaxed into her run, smiling inside.

"Good, isn't it?" asked her father beside her. She knew it was him, and she could hear that he was smiling too.

"I think I could do this for ever," Lottie told him breathlessly.

There was a tinge of sadness in his voice as he replied. "I thought that too, Lottie, I thought that too."

They slowed gradually, to a canter, then a

walk, then they stood, staring out through the leafless winter trees, across a shining midnight lake.

Still now, Lottie shook out her golden mane – it seemed she was a golden unicorn, unlike her father's silver – and admired its silky curls. It smelled good too, like Christmas spices. She cast a satisfied look back over her smooth coat, and flicked her waterfall of a tail. She looked like she had been polished.

"You're very beautiful," her father told her. "So tall. I've been away a long time. . ." He was smiling again, but a little sadly.

"Is it nice, to be a unicorn?" Lottie asked, wondering if she could stay. No more questions, only running under the moonlight.

"No." Her father was silent for a moment. "It's wonderful. But it isn't what we're meant to be, Lottie. Do you really want to leave everyone behind?"

Lottie blinked, long, golden lashes, flicking over her deep brown eyes. "No. Not Mum, and Sofie. Ruby. Even Danny. I couldn't."

"Exactly. You should always go back."

"Are you coming back?" Lottie asked hopefully.

"I'm trying, Lottie, I promise. It's hard."

45

The quiet moonlight faded, replaced by a groaning engine noise and a stinging, salty wind.

Now she was on a boat – no, a ship. A large one that smelled strange, like car exhaust but worse. She guessed it was the engine. There was a strong undertone of fish too. She was leaning over the side-rail, staring down at the grey water.

She could feel him standing beside her, but he didn't speak. Maybe he didn't know she was there.

Carefully, shyly, wondering if he would disappear as soon as she looked, Lottie glanced up.

Her father!

Really him this time, not the strange, silvery-white unicorn she'd seen before. Lottie's heart jumped, and she reached out her hand, hesitantly stroking the sleeve of his yellow oilskin jacket.

He couldn't feel her. Lottie sighed. It had been the same when she'd visited her mother in Paris once, walking through a magical door that Sofie had found in the pet shop. It had led them out into another shop, full of glittering birds flying free about a painted ceiling. A Paris pet shop, only a few streets from her mother's flat.

When she and Sofie had climbed the fire escape

and sneaked in through her mother's kitchen window, Lottie had rushed to hug her. Seeing her mum crying because she was missing her so much, Lottie'd forgotten that she wasn't meant to be there, that her mum would be full of questions. Lottie had only thought of holding her. But her mother couldn't tell she was there. Lottie was sure she'd felt *something*, but she and Sofie had been invisible, like ghosts. It was a good thing, really; it would have been so hard to explain how she'd got there – impossible, probably. But she had wanted a proper hug, all the same.

Now her father couldn't feel her either. It meant she wasn't really there, Lottie supposed. Still keeping her fingers on him – did she think he was going to float away? – Lottie took a little step backwards and looked up. Her father was very tall. She'd vaguely remembered that about him, but she'd censored it from her baby memories, thinking that he was tall only because she was so small. He still was, though. He was very tanned, much more so than Uncle Jack, who liked to say he was a troglodyte, hiding away from sunshine in his shop. Lottie supposed that if he'd been in India, or somewhere close to India, anyway, then he would be tanned. His hair was still black and curly, like hers, with just the odd silvery, wiry thread here and there.

His hands, folded on his arms as he leaned on the rail, had long, thin fingers, just like Lottie's. She caught her breath, staring at them. Daddy. She hadn't thought she remembered much, but she remembered those hands, making paper aeroplanes for her, doing the actions of the silly baby songs she liked to sing. Lottie moved her hand from his sleeve and laid it over the long fingers, dragging up all her love and hope, and sending it through her skin to speak to him.

He blinked. But that was all. He might just have had dry eyes from the sea wind.

Lottie sighed. At least he was on a boat. That had to be good, didn't it? He was travelling. Surely that meant he was coming home? The unicorn had said he was trying. This dream had to be a message, to show he was on his way back to her.

It was so frustrating, not being able to talk to him. Lottie almost wished he was a unicorn again – at least then he'd be able to see her, wouldn't he? And they could talk?

She almost wished it, but not quite. Seeing the real him was so amazing. He looked so like all those photographs. Like a taller, skinnier Uncle

Jack. It was like seeing a fading memory come alive again. She couldn't let it go, even if he couldn't talk to her.

Her father turned round and leaned against the rail, now staring up into the sky. He muttered something that Lottie couldn't quite hear, and she pressed in close against him, staring at his lips, willing him to say it again.

"She's after me. I can feel her coming. I don't know what she wants." He shook his head wearily. "What if she finds what I'm searching for?" He pressed his hands against his eyes, muttering angrily. "What *am* I searching for? I can't see, I can't see. Where are they all?"

Lottie put her arms round him, wishing he knew she was there. He had to be talking about Pandora, she was sure. Well, that answered her question. Pandora wasn't going to leave them alone. But she wasn't just coming back for Lottie. Now that she knew Lottie's dad was still alive, she was going after him instead.

4

Lottie woke up shaking, her hands stretching out to keep hold of her father, but he slipped away from her with sleep.

"What's the matter?" Sofie asked, wriggling grumpily as Lottie woke her, and Lottie suddenly realized that she and her father had been alone in the dream. Since Lottie and Sofie had bonded, Lottie hardly ever dreamed without Sofie there too.

"I was with my dad," she murmured to Sofie, watching her yawn and stretch in the half-light.

Sofie stopped mid-stretch and padded up the bed closer to her. "I do not understand. I was asleep. How could you go without me?"

The words were accusing, but Sofie's voice was somehow worse. She didn't sound as though she was trying to make Lottie feel guilty – she sounded lost, and bewildered, and desperately hurt.

"I don't know," Lottie told Sofie flatly. She knew that she should be conciliatory, comforting Sofie, reassuring her. But half her mind was still on that ship, staring out at the huge amount of sky and sea, and trying to make her father see her.

Sofie gave a pitiful little whine and went down to the end of the bed, where she tucked her nose under her paws, as though she was trying to hide.

Lottie lifted her head slowly. "Sofie, I'm sorry, I really don't know why you didn't come with me. I didn't mean it to happen that way. I just had a dream! Please don't be angry with me." She sighed wearily. She didn't feel as though she'd actually slept at all.

"'M not angry," Sofie muttered, from under her paws.

"Well, upset, then."

"You left me behind."

"I didn't mean to!" Lottie wailed, and jumped as Danny thumped on the wall from his bedroom next door to tell her to stop making that awful noise at this hour of the morning.

"We should go back to sleep. You have school."

And Sofie turned her back on Lottie, and when Lottie tried to reach her mind, she was met by a soft, blank fog that screamed *sleep*, in a most unsleepy way.

When Lottie woke up again, Uncle Jack's shout dragging her out of a shallow, restless sleep, Sofie was gone. Lottie threw on her school uniform and clattered down the stairs anxiously.

Sofie was drinking coffee in the kitchen. There were coffee bubbles on her nose, but she didn't have her usual first-caffeine-hit-of-the-day expression of bliss. Her whiskers had a decided droop. When she saw Lottie watching her from the doorway, she shook her ears briskly and tried to look unconcerned.

"Are you OK?" Lottie whispered, grabbing a glass and some juice, and sitting down next to her.

"Of course. Why would I not be?" Sofie asked airily.

Lottie didn't know what to say to break through her don't-care front, but she desperately wanted to, because she was sure Sofie did care, very much. "I have to get to school," she sighed. "I'll see you later. Will you try and help me with this calling spell, for the rabbit? Please?"

Sofie stared into her coffee. "Very well," she muttered ungraciously.

Lottie walked to meet Ruby at the bridge more slowly than she should have done. She was trying to work out why Sofie was being so grumpy about helping this rabbit. Did she really just not like rabbits? But Tabitha was a cat, and Sofie hated cats! It didn't make sense. And why had Sofie not been in her dream last night? All Lottie could think was that it was because they had quarrelled with each other just before she went to sleep. Had it really made that much difference? They'd disagreed with each other before. Though mostly only over who got the last chocolate. Lottie had been sure that Sofie being her familiar meant they would always be together – they were part of each other. That couldn't stop! Or at least, she hoped it couldn't. . .

Lottie kicked moodily through the autumn leaves and stomped on to the bridge to meet Ruby.

"Hey. Good morning to you too." Ruby grinned. She was wearing a mad red woolly hat with a huge pompom that clashed with her red curls so badly it looked really good. Lottie wished she had the guts to wear something like that.

"What's up?" Ruby asked as they walked on.

"Sofie's in a mood with me. I had another dream-visit from my dad last night, and I did it without her. She thinks I left her behind on purpose."

"And you didn't?" Ruby checked.

Lottie gave a short little laugh. "Nope. I didn't even know *I* was going. I couldn't have left her if I'd tried. She just didn't come."

"Did he tell you anything more? Was he still, um, a unicorn?" Ruby was a bit doubtful about the whole unicorn thing, but Lottie could see why. She didn't understand it properly herself.

"He was both. He started off as a unicorn, but then I saw the real him." Lottie smiled for the first time that morning. "I think he's coming home, Ruby. He was on a ship. But he didn't know I was there. And he thinks someone's chasing him. Her, he said. It has to be Pandora, doesn't it?"

"I guess so." Ruby shuddered. "Great. Just what we need. But it's good news, Lottie, isn't it? That your dad's coming home? You just don't sound as happy as I thought you would."

Lottie sighed. "I wish he'd recognized me, that's all. When he was on the ship, he couldn't even see me. And I'm really worried about Sofie. And that poor rabbit." She glanced back over her shoulder. They couldn't quite see the pet shop from here, but she knew the rabbit was close by, still staring at the wall behind his cage, she was sure. "We have to get him away from there," she muttered to Ruby.

"Did you try the spell that Ariadne suggested? Didn't it work?"

"I couldn't do it; Sofie disappeared last night. I was really cross with her. I think that might be why I went on that dream-journey without her, because I was still cross. And I really need her to help with the spell. Especially if he isn't a magic rabbit; it'll be even harder then." Lottie frowned. "Ruby, do you think Uncle Jack's right, and rabbits don't mind being shut up? Ones who aren't magical, I mean? Uncle Jack didn't seem to care as much when he thought it was just any old rabbit. Sofie certainly didn't. Why should magic animals be more important?"

Ruby wrinkled her nose. "Maybe magic animals feel things more?" she suggested, shrugging. "But you're right, it doesn't seem fair. Poor old thing. Lottie. . ." Ruby hesitated, and lowered her voice. They were getting close to school, and the street was busy with children hurrying along. "Maybe we should just steal him?"

Lottie stared at her, trying to work out if she was serious. "Do you mean it?"

"Well, I bet we could," Ruby said thoughtfully. "I don't think it would be that difficult, if we watched the shop and waited till she went out to the back. It didn't look like the sort of shop that had security cameras, did it? And the cage wasn't locked."

"But it's . . . well . . . *wrong*. . ." Lottie said helplessly.

"It's wrong to be cruel to animals, like you said," Ruby retorted. "Anyway. If the spell doesn't work, that's what I think we should do."

Lottie followed her friend through the school gates, thinking, not for the first time, that Ruby was ever so much braver than she was. She saw what she thought was right and did it, even if it meant doing something wrong along the way.

It was very brave – but Lottie hoped wholeheartedly that the spell would work after all. Stealing would be their last resort.

As they walked into the classroom, someone shoved Lottie, and she fell against the door frame, yelping as her shoulder hit the wood. Ruby, who was in front, shot back and grabbed her and hauled her up, glaring at the person behind.

"Oh, Lottie, I'm so sorry, I slipped," Zara Martin said sweetly, and she picked up Lottie's bag for her.

Lottie stared angrily into Zara's eyes, deep, dark-blue eyes, presently wide with innocence. She was a pink-cheeked, brown-haired, angelic-looking girl, always surrounded by a gang of friends who hung on her every word.

Lottie looked at Zara's eyes and saw herself reflected in them, looking small and pale. *That's what she makes me*, Lottie thought. *That's where she wants me, anyway.* Then another thought flitted in: *Her eyes are hard, like glass mirrors.*

She smiled charmingly at Zara, and saw the reflection change, the washed-out look colouring to a true picture. Lottie had cast a strong spell on Zara a few weeks before, one that had shaken Zara's position as everyone's favourite, or at least, everyone's princess. Lottie was fairly sure no one in the class actually liked her that much. But she'd been alternately bullying and charming all of them since nursery school, and they'd grown into the habit of obedience.

Zara's pretty mouth twisted in a hard line as she realized Lottie wasn't scared of her. "Are you going to stand in the door all day?" she snapped.

Lottie walked slowly to her table, turning her back on Zara, even though that felt like a bad thing to do – like turning one's back on a snake about to strike.

"I told you that you shouldn't have let her forget what you did!" Ruby hissed, as Lottie sat down. "She's as bad as ever!"

Lottie shook her head. "No, she doesn't scare me like she used to. She's definitely rattled. She knows that no one worships her quite as much as they used to, but she doesn't know why. And she hates not knowing." Lottie couldn't help sounding a touch smug, but then she had been very proud of that spell.

Lottie smiled to herself. As Zara had pushed her, she'd felt a dart of worry from Sofie, responding to Lottie falling. Sofie might be upset with her, but they were still joined, and Sofie still cared about her. She thought lovingly of Sofie, and received back a message of a sleepy dog curled up on the old armchair in the kitchen. Apparently the shop was irritatingly busy, and Sofie didn't want to be disturbed. *Pay attention, Lottie,* she scolded, yawning and turning round more comfortably on the chair. *You are supposed to be working.*

Lottie's smugness was nothing compared to Sofie's.

Because Lottie had got ahead with her homework, it meant that as soon as she got home from school she could start work on the spell. Lottie grinned to herself as she dumped her school bag in the kitchen. She supposed Mrs Laurence had to be right occasionally. She was always lecturing year six about not leaving their work till the last minute.

Sofie was still in the armchair, and Lottie suspected that she might not have moved all day, except perhaps to consume a small snack or three at lunch time.

"I know you aren't asleep," Lottie told her firmly. "Come on, we need to go and try out that spell."

Sofie rolled on to her back and waved her paws in the air pathetically. Her shiny black nails sparkled. "I am hungry," she moaned. "Magic is most fatiguing. I will need chocolate. Lots of chocolate." A bright, roguish eye peeped at Lottie, before she closed them both again, so as to look suitably weary.

"We've run out of the last box from Mum,"

Lottie told her. "But I bought you a bar on the way home from school, OK?"

Sofie sat up very quickly. "Milk or dark?"

"The kind with the nutty stuff in the middle."

"Oh, very well then." Sofie leaped lightly down from the chair and pranced off to the stairs. "I hope it is a *large* bar; this spell sounded very difficult," she called back.

When Lottie reached her room, Sofie was sitting expectantly on the bed, the very tip of her bright-pink tongue sticking out. She stared hopefully at Lottie's pockets.

Lottie pulled out the bar of chocolate and unwrapped it, breaking off a large piece.

Sofie leaned towards it hungrily.

"Just this one bit," Lottie told her, "and the rest after we've done the spell. Or at least tried to. OK?"

Sofie nodded vigorously and accepted the chocolate with a rapturous expression, closing her eyes and sighing deeply. It lasted about ten seconds, then her eyes snapped open and she barked, "More!"

"No! I told you, no more until we've done the spell." Lottie frowned.

"Oh, Lottie, just one more piece," Sofie pleaded, her head on one side, fluttering her eyelashes.

"No! You can lay on all the charm you want, I won't give you any." Lottie folded her arms firmly and glared at Sofie. She could feel that Sofie was trying to persuade her with magic. Her fingers itched to open the paper wrapper again. "Sofie, stop it! That's rude!"

Sofie huffed crossly. "I am *very* hungry," she complained. "One little piece would not have hurt. Come on, then, let us do this silly spell, if we must."

Lottie sat down beside her, putting the chocolate in the drawer of her bedside table.

"We have to think about the rabbit. Picture him, Uncle Jack said." She put her hand on Sofie's back, feeling the warmth of her fur, and closed her eyes hopefully, waiting for the images to flood into her mind. They didn't.

"I cannot picture him," Sofie complained. "I did not see him."

Lottie sighed. "Can't you just think of a rabbit? He was grey, with sweet twitchy ears."

Sofie scowled. "No. I do not like rabbits. Silly little white fluffy tails they have."

"Sofie, I need you to help me, please," Lottie begged. "I can't do this without you." She was half buttering Sofie up, but half of her really meant it.

She needed Sofie's power, and her familiarity with magic, to push the spell out of her mind and into the real world.

Sofie smiled. Dogs can't smile in quite the same way as humans, they don't have the lips for it, but Sofie managed. It was a supremely satisfied little smirk. "Oh, very well," she said carelessly. "If you really cannot manage without me."

Lottie closed her eyes again, staring into the sparkling darkness behind her eyelids, and tried to remember the little grey rabbit. It was the expression in his eyes that she remembered most clearly, the way that at first there had been no life in them; then, when he saw that Lottie was actually interested in him, the look of amazement he'd given her as he turned round to see her properly.

Lightly stroking Sofie's back, she imagined the softer fur of the rabbit, and waited for Sofie's strong magic to help her. "Rabbits!" she whispered to Sofie, trying to concentrate still.

Reluctantly, slowly, a surge of magic from Sofie joined her own. Lottie began to build a picture of a rabbit, a little grey rabbit, with sad brown eyes, floating in the air in front of them, like the image she had made of Zara. When he was there, and real, she would be able to call to him. But he was still too misty and wobbly, and the colour wasn't quite right. She drew more of Sofie's magic. Soft, chocolatey brown fur. Chocolate eyes.

Chocolate whiskers.

"He had white whiskers," Lottie murmured to herself. But the whiskers stayed obstinately chocolate, and the rabbit had a white-chocolate tail, and white-chocolate eyes. . .

Lottie's eyes flew open. "Sofie! This isn't an Easter bunny! It's a real rabbit, not one made of chocolate."

"I cannot help it," Sofie muttered sulkily, her black eyes flashing with crossness. "I am hungry, and I want that chocolate, and I do not know what the rabbit looks like. I know what chocolate looks like. If you want me to help, you will have to feed me properly," she added, with her nose in the air. "If you fed me properly, I might have fur as soft as a rabbit's."

Lottie blinked at her. "Are you jealous?" she asked in amazement.

"Of course not!" Sofie snapped, but she wouldn't look at Lottie, and her voice was too loud.

"Sofie, is that why you won't try to do this properly, because you don't want us to rescue the rabbit? You're jealous of him?"

Sofie said nothing. She looked mulishly out of the window.

"That's stupid!" Lottie burst out. "You don't need to be jealous! Sofie, I love you. Helping that rabbit escape from somewhere horrible isn't going to change that!"

Sofie's ears twitched when Lottie said she loved her, but she didn't move. Instead, she sent Lottie a fleeting glimpse of herself cuddling a rabbit (which was extremely ugly) while Sofie herself stood on her hind legs, sadly scratching at Lottie's knee with one trembling paw. Lottie was ignoring her.

"Oh, that's so unfair!" Lottie burst out. She glared at Sofie, who still wouldn't look at her. "Fine. If that's how you're going to be." Lottie closed her eyes again and leaned back against the wall. She wasn't as skilled with mind-pictures as Sofie, and she needed to concentrate.

This is what it's like for the rabbit, Sofie. This is what it might be like for you, if you had an owner who didn't love you.

Sofie was lying on a cushion in the corner of a kitchen, watching with nervous eyes as a little girl sorted through a basket of doll's clothes.

"There! I knew it was the right size." She seized

triumphantly on a small pink dress and a bonnet, and flung her doll to the floor. "Come here, Sofie!"

Sofie yelped and shot off her cushion, racing into the hallway, and the little girl hurtled after her, shrieking. "Sofie! Bad dog! Come back, come back here this minute!"

Sofie raced into the living room and scooted under the sofa, pressing herself to the back. She hid there, trembling and whimpering under her breath, while the little girl stamped and cried and begged her to come out.

"Crystal! It's time for school, come and put your coat on!" Another voice called from the hallway, and the little girl got up, grumbling, and Sofie heard her stomping out of the room.

She crept to the front of the sofa, listening cautiously. If they really were off to school, she would have a few hours' grace until Crystal came back. She would be able to relax, and sleep without having to keep one eye open.

She heard Crystal's mother in the hall, asking, "Did you remember to feed the dog, Crystal, and let her out?"

"Yes," Crystal told her, not even listening.

She hadn't, of course, Sofie thought hungrily. Had she been fed last night? She wasn't sure. She was used to going hungry. When they did remember to feed her, they opened little tins that smelled strange, but she ate them. She preferred the smell of her owners' food, but she wasn't allowed it; she only got it occasionally when Crystal didn't want something and she would feed it to Sofie under the table. It was usually vegetables, but even so it was nice to have a change from food that was always brown.

She wriggled out from under the sofa and limped back to her cushion. She had banged her paw on the door when she was running away from the pink dress. She wondered sadly if Crystal's mother might take her for a walk today. It was sunny, and it would be so nice to be outside, even if her paw did hurt.

Quietly, Sofie curled up on her cushion, burying her nose under her paws, and trying to dream of another home, a home where she was loved.

Lottie opened her eyes and looked at Sofie, who was staring back at her in horror.

"You want me to have another home?" Sofie whispered. "You want me to belong to someone else?"

Lottie had never seen her look so woebegone. She looked like the dream-Sofie cowering under the sofa, her ears drooping. Lottie sighed and reached out a hand to Sofie. But Sofie drew back, trembling.

"Sofie! Of course I don't. I just wanted you to see – it isn't fair! Why shouldn't that rabbit have a home where he's loved too?"

"You do not love me any more," Sofie said, with dismal certainty. "You want a rabbit to be your familiar instead. So he can jump out of hats. I am too big for a hat."

"No!" Lottie groaned. "You aren't listening! It isn't about you, Sofie, it's about the rabbit. I do love you, but—"

"Everything is about the rabbit," Sofie said quietly, as she slipped off the bed and padded to the door with her tail trailing.

"Oh well, if you're not even going to listen to me," Lottie said crossly. "Fine! Go on then." And she watched angrily as Sofie went out of the room and pattered off down the stairs, her claws slipping and scrabbling, as though she wasn't concentrating on where she was putting her feet. Lottie grabbed the iPod her mum had sent her and lay on the bed, filling her mind with the music, even though she didn't hear it, just so that she couldn't feel the gap where Sofie had been.

"Lottie, dinner!" Uncle Jack was yelling up the stairs. "Danny, get off that computer, dinner time!"

Lottie got up, telling herself firmly that she was not going to give in. She was not going to let Sofie get away with this. The little dog was being horribly selfish, and Lottie wasn't going to stop trying to rescue the rabbit, even if she wouldn't help. Even if she wouldn't talk to Lottie. It was going to be hard, though. Lottie relied on Sofie being there. That constant comfort and reassurance – and frequent telling off, but at least before she'd always felt that Sofie was on her side.

She stalked down the stairs and marched into the kitchen, expecting to see Sofie perched at the table, her china bowl in front of her, questioning Uncle Jack about the exact recipe he had used to make the dinner and most likely telling him it was wrong. She always wanted more garlic in everything, and she persisted in calling all the ingredients by their French names, which confused him no end.

But Sofie's chair was empty.

Lottie stood in the doorway, feeling horribly cold all at once. "Where's Sofie?" she asked.

Uncle Jack turned round from the pan of pasta sauce he was stirring and gazed at her in surprise. "I thought she was with you. You went upstairs together when you came in from school, didn't you?"

"Yes, but. . ." Lottie didn't want to admit they'd argued. "She came downstairs again," she muttered. "We sort of – she was cross with me."

"I haven't seen her." Uncle Jack looked worried, and as Danny wandered in from the little office where the computer was kept, he added, "Have you seen Sofie, Dan? She's disappeared."

Danny shook his head vaguely.

Uncle Jack frowned. "It isn't like her to miss food. I hope she hasn't gone off to do anything silly. Can you call her, Lottie?"

Lottie had promised herself she wouldn't make the first move. She was right, and she knew it, and Sofie wasn't being fair. Sofie could apologize. But now she was worried, and she sent out a gentle little call, opening her mind to Sofie hopefully.

But there was nothing. Sofie was gone.

5

Panicking, Lottie ran out into the night to look for Sofie. It was November, and very dark already, and as Lottie looked wildly up and down the street, she could only see the small circles of pavement lit by the street lamps.

Danny appeared in the doorway behind her. "Has she really gone?" he asked, disbelievingly. "It's freezing out here, and you know she hates the cold. She's probably hiding in the shop somewhere."

Lottie nodded gratefully, desperate for any shred of hope. She closed her eyes and searched for Sofie's velvet warmth in the shop. Then again, and again. She could feel the tiny magical pulses of all the mice, even Henrietta, the homing mouse, a deceptive little creature who was invisible whenever she wanted to be. She could sense Selina and Sarafan, prowling round and round their pen, in case the locks had changed since they last looked. She could see Giles the hamster in her mind, running and puffing on his wheel. But Sofie wasn't there. She was nowhere, to Lottie.

Lottie looked up miserably at Danny. "She isn't there. She has to be out here somewhere, but I can't find her. I can't feel her at all, Danny! She's gone!"

"OK, OK, calm down. What did you say to her, Lottie? It can't have been anything that bad."

Danny's rat, Septimus, poked his head out of Danny's hood to hear too.

"I wanted her to help me with a spell," Lottie told them, staring out into the darkness, hoping to see a little dog running along the street homewards. "Sofie didn't want to; she was jealous because I was trying to save a rabbit from that horrible pet shop by the bridge. She kept messing the spell up, and I told her off. I – I tried to show her what it would be like to have an owner who didn't love her, but she took it the wrong way and thought I meant *I* didn't love her, and I really do!"

"Lottie, Sofie knows that," Septimus said calmly. "She may be upset at the moment, but in the cold light of day she'll realize what you meant."

"I'm not worried about the cold light of day, I'm worried about her being out here now, when it's night-time and it's actually cold!" Lottie muttered.

"Sofie is resourceful," Septimus pointed out. "Extremely so. I wouldn't put it past her to have found a nice old lady who's a soft touch for a cute little dog. Probably within about five minutes of walking out of the shop she was sitting on someone else's sofa eating someone else's sausages. Excuse me, *saucissons*. You know what she's like, Lottie. She can really work those eyes."

Lottie sniffed, and nodded. "I know. I suppose you're right. But I don't want her to have to. I want her home with me. Pandora's out there, and she knows Sofie now. What if she finds her? What if Sofie doesn't come back?"

"She will," Septimus said firmly. But he glanced quickly up at Danny as he said it, and he climbed out of Danny's hood and on to his shoulder, to be closer to him, as though he didn't like where this conversation was going.

"I might have driven her away," Lottie gulped. "Maybe for ever. . . If she really thinks I don't love her any more. She won't talk to me, Danny, I can't feel her!"

"Have you . . . umm . . . grovelled?" Septimus

enquired. "Sofie is very proud, Lottie. She won't want to make the first move. You might need to beg." He looked at her thoughtfully.

Lottie sighed. "You're right. I thought she was being mean, but maybe I was a bit over the top. Look, can you tell Uncle Jack I don't want any tea? I need to go and try calling her again. And I'll beg, Sep. Thanks."

Up in her room, Lottie stared out of the window. Grace's Pet Shop was a tall, thin building, and she could see over the roofs of Netherbridge, up to Netherbridge Hill. She shuddered. Hopefully Sofie wasn't up there. Lottie focused on the stars, so clear that they seemed to hang in the sky like Christmas decorations, and thought of Sofie.

Please, please, please, she begged. *I'm sorry, Sofie. I should have been nicer. I was worried about this rabbit, and I didn't think that that would make you upset. You don't need to be, honestly. I love you. You're the most special thing. You know that, you must know that. Please, Sofie, come back. . .*

Lottie waited, gazing hopefully out at the stars. But they only glittered coldly, and there was no answering voice in her mind. Sofie wasn't there.

Since she and Sofie had discovered their magical

bond, Lottie hadn't spent a night without Sofie curled at the end of her bed. Or in her bed, sometimes, if the night was cold. Sofie liked to sleep with her head on the pillow, next to Lottie's. Lottie hadn't thought she'd miss Sofie's big ears flapping in her face.

She got up the next morning miserable and lonely, and the feeling didn't go even when she met Ruby to walk to school.

"You look awful, what's wrong?" Ruby demanded as soon as she saw her.

Lottie didn't even bother to protest. She explained what had happened, and Ruby's face fell.

"Oh, Lottie, no! You've no idea where she is?"

"I can't feel her at all. Can we not talk about it, for a bit? I don't want to." Lottie hardly spoke on the way, but at the same time she resented Ruby's answering silence. She'd told Ruby she didn't want to talk about it, but Ruby's horrified agreement just made her feel worse.

Mrs Laurence had decided to make them all draw maps of their houses that morning, which was good, because it was something Lottie could do with half her brain, and she didn't have to talk to anyone. But it also meant she was free to think miserable thoughts.

Dad's disappeared. Who knows where he is, or if he's even really coming back, she worried to herself. *Mum would rather be in a different country than be with me. Uncle Jack only has me at the shop because he has to. And now I've even driven Sofie away! What's wrong with me?*

By morning break she was so unhappy she just wanted to snap at someone, and unfortunately, it was Ruby who spoke to her first.

They were sitting huddled on a bench, staring glumly at the boys playing football, when Ruby asked, "Lottie, I know you said you didn't want to talk about it, but have you tried looking for Sofie?"

"What sort of stupid question is that?" Lottie snarled. "Of course I have!"

Ruby looked hurt, but she carried on. "I mean looking for her properly. Not with magic. Going out to look for her."

"She's a magical dog, so I looked for her with magic, all right? You don't understand."

Ruby shrugged. "OK, then," she muttered. "Be like that."

Lottie glared at her. "Oh, sorry. I'm the one with the lost dog. Aren't I allowed to be upset?"

Ruby glared back. "Upset yes, rude no. I was only trying to help."

"Well, don't."

"Fine, I won't!"

"Good!" Lottie snapped.

Ruby got up, and leaned down for her parting shot. "If this is how you treat your friends, Lottie, I'm not surprised Sofie left." Then she turned on her heel and stalked away.

Lottie gasped. It felt like Ruby had hit her in the stomach, and she couldn't breathe properly for a moment. Mostly because she was worried that Ruby was right. Had she driven Sofie away? As she watched Ruby stomping across the playground, hands shoved in her pockets, her face sunk into her scarf, obviously glad to get away from her, Lottie thought unhappily that she must have done. And now she had just done it to her best friend too.

Lottie had her eyes fixed on the retreating figure so closely that she didn't notice someone leaning over her shoulder, until Zara whispered in her ear.

"She doesn't look very happy, Lottie. Did you have a fight?"

"Go away," Lottie muttered.

"Go awa-aaay!" Zara mimicked, and Bethany and the others giggled worshipfully.

Zara sat down on the bench next to Lottie and

smiled sweetly at her. "Tell me what happened, Lottie, maybe I can help you two make it up. After all, it would be so sad if the two most unpopular girls in the class weren't friends, wouldn't it? You might start wanting to hang around with us!" She snickered.

Lottie stared at her disgustedly. "When hell freezes over. I don't even want to *see* you, let alone talk to you." It was amazing how being totally miserable made you brave, she thought. *Even after the spell, I'd normally be more scared of her than this.*

A tiny frown crossed Zara's face for a second. Lottie answering back was not in her plan.

"It's a good thing you've got that little rat of a dog, Lottie, since you haven't got any other friends," she hissed, upping her nastiness level a bit.

Lottie lifted her head and looked Zara full in the face, showing her teeth, rather like Sofie did when she was angry. "Don't you dare talk about her like that!" she yelled. Hardly even stopping to think, she lifted her hand and smacked Zara round the face.

Zara stared at her in amazement, and Lottie stared back. She was quite amazed too. Zara slowly lifted one hand to her cheek, as though she was checking it was still there. "You really shouldn't have done that," she whispered.

Lottie smiled at her. There was a wonderful freedom in having done something really, really stupid. She just didn't care any more. "Why not?" She beamed at Zara. "It felt brilliant. Maybe I should do it again."

Zara grabbed her coat and pulled her upright. "Bethany, help me!" she snapped, and together they flung Lottie back against the bench, bruising her arm.

Lottie sprang back up. Even though she couldn't feel Sofie at the moment, it was as though she was drawing on her fighting spirit. Sofie would have loved this. She would have been cheering. Lottie was almost sure she could feel her, watching, just out of reach of Lottie's mind. She ran at Zara, pushing her to the ground, and sat on her. Bethany was standing there looking helpless. She and Anya made a half-hearted attempt to pull Lottie off, but neither of them wanted to get hurt, and they backed off when Lottie shoved them away.

Then Zara started to fight back. She scratched at Lottie's cheek, raking her nails across her face, and Lottie yelped and scrambled away.

"Lottie!" Ruby was rushing back across the

playground now, and she hauled Lottie up, both of them stumbling back, staring at Zara, who was spitting and ranting on the ground, yelling at Bethany to help her up. "I can't believe you hit her!"

"Me neither," Lottie murmured.

By now Zara was up again. She shoved at Lottie furiously, Ruby shoved her back – and that was just when Anya came back with Mrs Laurence.

"Girls! Are you fighting?" the teacher demanded in a shocked voice.

"Lottie and Ruby are picking on me, Mrs Laurence," Zara whimpered. "Lottie pushed me over, and she hit me."

"Lottie, is this true?" Mrs Laurence said sternly.

"Well, yes, but. . ."

"She and Ruby ganged up on me," Zara said, sniffing.

"But. . ." Lottie wondered how Mrs Laurence managed not to see her scratched face, as she ranted on about how disappointed she was with Lottie and Ruby. She looked disbelievingly at Ruby, who shrugged.

"Zara's had *years* of practice. Just try to look sorry," she whispered.

Mrs Laurence put them in after-school detention –

which meant she would have to phone Uncle Jack and Ruby's parents.

Ruby grinned as they followed the furious teacher back into school, leaving Zara gloating to her mates. "I really hope my mum's painting. She hates it when people phone. Mrs Laurence will end up apologizing to *her*."

"Won't she be cross?" Lottie asked, wondering what Uncle Jack was going to think. He knew that Zara had bullied her before, so hopefully he'd believe Lottie's side of the story.

"Oh, probably, but she'll stick up for me to Mrs Laurence."

Certainly, when Mrs Laurence came out of the office five minutes later, she was decidedly pink, and her eyes were snapping with anger. "Right, you two. An hour's detention after school. You can write about why fighting is never the answer to any problem."

Lottie and Ruby nodded, and tried to look apologetic. But as Mrs Laurence strode away, Ruby put an arm round Lottie. "What did Zara say to you? I've never seen you look like that before. And when you smacked her, oh, Lottie, I wanted to cheer. It was bliss."

Lottie grinned for a minute. "It felt good too. She

called Sofie a rat, and with Sofie gone, I couldn't bear it." Her voice wobbled. "So I hit her." Lottie sniffed, and added, wobbling even more, "I just wish Sofie could have seen!"

"I'm sorry you got dragged into that," Lottie told Ruby as they walked home in the gathering dark after their detention. "Mrs Laurence was really unfair."

Ruby grinned. "I told you that you shouldn't have let everyone forget the spell-picture you made of Zara. Mrs Laurence has gone back to thinking she's an angel."

"Mmm. But everyone would have known it was something to do with me, and how would we explain it? Aliens?" Lottie sighed. "It's tempting, though. I really don't know how Zara does it.

"Like I said, years of practice. And she has no shame and no feelings. Anyway, forget her. We don't have to see her until tomorrow, and then I can just relive you smacking her all over again. Are you going back home to do another search for Sofie?"

Lottie shook her head. "No, I can't find her by magic; I think she's hiding herself. You know what you were saying earlier, when I was horrible?

About finding her the other way, actually going out and looking? I think I need to do that."

"It's getting dark," Ruby pointed out, shivering a little. "You can't go now."

Lottie shrugged. "Well, I've got to go home first and see what Uncle Jack says about the detention, but I have to do something. I can't sit around and just wait for her to come back. What if she doesn't? Or even if she does, and she thinks I didn't even try to find her?"

Ruby looked thoughtful. "Mmm. I see what you mean. Have you got a photo of her?"

Lottie blinked, surprised. "Yes, lots. You know what a show-off Sofie is, she loves having her photo taken."

"Then I think we should make LOST posters in the computer and put them up round the town. I could stick some up for you on the way home. Mum texted me to say she thinks Mrs Laurence is a twit, and was Zara still bullying you, so I don't reckon I need to go home and grovel." She fluttered her eyelashes hopefully at Lottie. "That's if you want me, of course?"

Lottie hugged her. "You know, when you stormed off earlier on, I couldn't believe I'd just had a fight with you as well. I was sitting there thinking I'd lost everybody, even you. That's when Zara turned up – she chose just the wrong moment. That's why I hit her."

"I'm an inspiration," Ruby said happily.

6

Lottie got up early the next morning, and left for school with a pile of posters and roll of the parcel tape that Uncle Jack used for wrapping orders he sent by post. She was glad to get out of the shop without seeing her uncle. He hadn't been cross about the detention; in fact, he'd offered again to come into school to talk to Mrs Laurence about Zara. Lottie couldn't think of anything worse. He was worried about Sofie, though. All last evening, he'd been thinking of places she might be, and asking Lottie to use her bond with Sofie to search. She'd tried so many times, and each time she'd found nothing and felt more helpless. Ariadne had come round to help, and the worry in her eyes every time they found nothing had made Lottie feel sick. She didn't want to face another barrage of suggestions this morning.

Usually if she was going out early for something, she'd ask Sofie to tell Uncle Jack, she thought sadly, and left her message with Horace instead.

The grumpy old parrot eyed her posters. "Spelled all the words right, have you? Mmmm. Good girl."

Lottie blinked. Horace was never nice. Her eyes filled with tears as she unlocked the shop door. If Horace was missing an opportunity to tell her off, it probably meant he'd given up on Sofie ever coming back.

"I'm going to find her, you know," she told him, almost angrily.

"That's the spirit." Giles the hamster nodded. "Off you go, Lottie dear."

"Go get her, Lottie!" It was Fred, dancing up and down with his friend Peach in front of their cage. They twirled their tails together like ribbons on a maypole and spun round, singing, "Lottie, Lottie, Lottie!"

Lottie walked through the misty streets, taping her posters to lamp posts and fences. When she saw a shop that was open, she asked them to put a poster in their window. The waiter at her and

Sofie's favourite café was just undoing the shutters when she went past. He was horrified when she told him, and took two posters. He adored Sofie, and always gave her extra biscuits with her *espresso*. He told Lottie she looked hungry, and gave her a croissant. Lottie nibbled it as she walked along, wishing Sofie was there to share it – she loved croissants.

Lottie circled back round so that she would end up by the bridge to meet Ruby as usual. She'd spotted a few posters that Ruby had put up the previous evening too. She walked past the dingy little pet shop, and stared in the window. She could just see the rabbit's cage. There was a small, greyish heap in one corner – the rabbit – curled up hopelessly. He looked even more unhappy than he had before. *Maybe I made things worse for him too,* Lottie thought miserably. *Making him think someone cared, and then just disappearing. I've got to get him away. Maybe Mum would send me some money to buy him . . . I'll try the spell again tonight. I was too worried about Sofie to try yesterday, but the rabbit doesn't know that. It isn't his fault.*

That evening, Lottie went up to her room, hearing a ghostly patter of claws on the stairs in front of her, and knowing that it was only in her mind. Wishful thinking. She felt so lonely – the idea of a complex spell with no help from Sofie was terrifying. She supposed she was being silly – it wasn't as if she was fighting against someone with this spell, as she had been against Pandora only a few days before. If it went wrong, she wouldn't be enslaved by a mad enchantress who hated her family. But somehow the thought of all that power out there, all that magic, was simply awful. What if she broke it? What if she tried to do something that wasn't allowed, and her magic simply disappeared? What if she turned herself purple?

Stop it! Lottie said to herself firmly. There was no reason it should go wrong, just because Sofie wasn't there. It would be harder, that was all. Good practice.

And anyway, she thought gloomily, she couldn't face being downstairs right now. Uncle Jack was still in a complete twitter over Sofie, as apparently he'd spent ages last night trying to search for her by magic too. He hadn't found so much as a whisker, and he was gobsmacked. Lottie suspected that he wanted to get Sofie back partly because he was desperate to know how she'd managed to hide herself so cleverly.

Lottie decided she needed something to look at, rather than just staring into the darkness. Something rabbity. . . She looked around her room, frowning, then jumped up, grabbing one of the animal magazines that she'd brought with her when she first moved to Grace's. She hadn't bothered buying them recently, not since she'd had real animals to look at – and talk to.

Eagerly she flicked through; she was sure she remembered an article on rabbits. At last she found it, a page covered in photos of rabbits gazing out at her. None of them looked exactly like the rabbit in the pet shop – he was a particularly lovely shade of soft silvery grey, Lottie realized now – but they would do. She picked the closest, a rabbit with a pretty grey coat and an endearingly pink nose, and tore the picture out. Then she sat holding it, staring into the paper eyes and hoping. . .

Lottie became aware of a smell. Not a very bad smell, just not quite fresh. As though someone hadn't bothered to clean out the cage quite as often as they should. And food that was enough, but the same all the time. Never even a scrap of carrot or fresh apple. And the loneliness. No one to talk to. No one even to touch.

Hello. . . she murmured quietly, still staring at the picture in her hand.

The rabbit's pink nose twitched, wrinkling the paper, and Lottie squeaked with excitement and shock. She hadn't expected that to happen. The rabbit squeaked back anxiously, and Lottie felt guilty. *I'm sorry, I didn't mean to frighten you. Do you remember me? I came to the shop before, with my friend. We were worried about you.*

The rabbit stared at her with big dark-brown eyes. The eyes glimmered with fear, but with intelligence too, Lottie was sure. Nothing like Sofie's, but even if this wasn't a rabbit that could talk, she was sure it could understand her.

Don't be scared. Please. Can you talk?

The rabbit nodded, very slightly. So slightly that Lottie almost thought she'd imagined it. *Don't you want to?* she asked.

The paper rabbit looked around. Its pretty grass and flowers background had changed to grubby cage bedding now. *Not safe*, it muttered cautiously, then it closed its eyes and hunched its shoulders, as though it expected the sky to fall in.

But we're only talking in our heads, Lottie reminded him. *No one can hear you.*

The rabbit frowned, the brown eyes looking

confused. Then he nodded, slowly. *Maybe*, he agreed in a whisper. *I'm not sure.*

What's your name? Lottie asked. *Do you have one?*

Barney, the rabbit whispered, still looking panicky.

Barney, I really want to get you out of that horrible shop. That would be good, wouldn't it? Lottie asked persuasively.

The rabbit nodded, his eyes suddenly brightening with hope.

If I call you, will you come? Lottie begged.

Barney blinked. *How?* he asked, honestly bewildered.

Lottie looked at him helplessly. *I'm not quite sure,* she admitted. *But I think it should just work — somehow. . .*

Barney looked at her with his head on one side, and blinked thoughtfully. *Do you by any chance have a dog?* he asked.

Lottie was so surprised that she dropped the picture, and when she scrabbled to pick it up again, it was only a paper rabbit, gazing foolishly from a grassy meadow. Barney had gone.

"Oh no! Stupid! What did I drop it for?" she wailed. It had been working, really working, and then she'd messed it up.

Why had Barney asked her that, of all things? Had he seen Sofie in her mind, somehow? Lottie supposed that anyone she tried to speak in thoughts with at the moment would be able to tell that Lottie had lost Sofie and desperately wanted her back. It must be all over her mind. She shouldn't have reacted so stupidly.

Sunk in gloom, she lay down on the bed, staring at the ceiling and thinking of Sofie. Sofie would have caught the paper for her when she dropped it, snapped at her until she'd got the thought connection back, and told the rabbit to stop fussing and just come. Sofie would have had it sorted in no time. *I need her back*, Lottie thought miserably. *I can't do all this without her. How am I going to get her back?* A tear rolled down her chin, and she brushed it away crossly. Sofie thought crying was silly, and it was.

"Lottie! Lottie!" Uncle Jack was yelling excitedly downstairs.

"What is it?" Lottie muttered back wearily, then, realizing he couldn't hear her, she heaved herself up and went out to the top of the stairs to say that she wasn't feeling well and she was going to bed.

Standing at the bottom of the stairs was Sofie.

Lottie wasn't sure afterwards how she'd got down them. She wouldn't have been surprised if someone had told her she'd just jumped from the top step.

"Sofie, Sofie, you came back. . ." Lottie hugged her lovingly, as Sofie wriggled with delight in her arms. "I thought you weren't coming back, I thought I'd made you leave for ever."

"You put posters up, with me on them," Sofie said smugly. "I saw lots of me, all over town. But Lottie, that was not my best picture. Why did you choose that one, hmm? My nose looked big. Which it is not."

"Where were you?" Lottie asked. "Were you safe? Where did you go?"

"A little girl found me – or I found her, perhaps. I slept in her playhouse, and she gave me her sandwiches. Marmite." Sofie wrinkled her nose disapprovingly.

Lottie tried hard not to look upset, but she felt terribly, terribly jealous. "Was she – nice?" she murmured.

Sofie shrugged. "She was a baby. *Very* little. But sweet." She put her head on one side and looked at Lottie slyly. "When *I* was jealous, Lottie, you were cross with me. You said I was being selfish. . ." She looked up at the ceiling, humming a little French tune to herself.

"I know, Sofie." Lottie leaned her head against the velvety wrinkles of Sofie's neck. "I've never had to share you, have I? And you have to share me a lot." She sat down on the stairs, glad that they led down into the passage and not straight into the shop where the others could hear her. "But you know that I don't have the same bond with Tabitha or Giles or any of the others, don't you? Even Fred?"

Sofie pressed her nose into the crook of Lottie's elbow, hard. Her voice was a little muffled. "I know. But you love everybody so much, Lottie. And you wanted another one. . . I am a jealous person." Sofie took a deep breath. "I am sorry," she said, rather grandly.

"I didn't want him for my own, Sofie, only for him not to be in that shop any more," Lottie promised.

"Yes, it was not a good place. Nobody should have to live there." Sofie shook her head disgustedly. "The smell!"

"Exactly, and no one ever talked to him, he was so— Sofie, how do you know? Did you go there?" Lottie held her out, looking at her in surprise, and Sofie wriggled expertly out of her grip.

"You had better come," she called over her shoulder, prancing into the shop.

Sitting on the counter, staring dazedly at a beautiful selection of vegetables – clearly Uncle Jack had raided the fridge – was Barney the rabbit.

Lottie gazed at him in amazement, and then looked down at Sofie. "Did you bring him?"

Sofie shrugged. "You wanted him, so I went and got him." She yawned, but she was watching Lottie out of one eye all the time.

"How?" Lottie gasped.

Sofie scrambled on to the window, then up to the stool, so she could put her paws up on the counter and hold court. "When I first went out of the shop, I did not mean to go anywhere in particular – I was upset and I wanted to run, that was all."

"I'm sorry," Lottie whispered, stroking her guiltily.

"It was that little dream-girl you showed me, Lottie. It was all so real. I could not help thinking that that was what you really wanted, for me to live with someone else. I spent the night in the playhouse, the nice little girl's playhouse, thinking perhaps I would have to find another home. And the next day, she had to go to school, but she came back and fed me biscuits, so I thought I might stay, even though the playhouse was cold. But then in the morning, I saw the pictures, and I knew you wanted me back. I could smell you on them, and you smelled sad. So – I thought I had better make you happy again. I had perhaps been a leetle bit selfish. So I brought you the rabbit."

"She said I had to come," Barney the rabbit put in, a piece of lettuce trailing rather foolishly from his mouth.

Sofie glared at him. "And you made a great fuss! You cannot have wanted to stay in that place. You should have just come at once, without all the silliness."

Barney stared at her, blinking nervously. He was clearly not a rabbit of very great brain. He nodded. "Yes, Sofie," he murmured politely.

Sofie frowned. "Mmm. Very well then."

"I still don't understand how you did it," Lottie said, pulling another stool up to the counter. "Was that horrible old woman there?"

"She went out to the back of the shop to have her lunch," Sofie explained. "I could smell her nasty sandwiches. So while she was gone I sneaked in and tried to persuade this idiot to go with me. But he just kept blinking at me, and saying he would not dare. He is a big coward!"

Barney nodded sadly. "Rabbits are," he agreed.

Sofie made an indescribable noise, something like *pffft*. It was a fairly clear opinion of rabbits. "Then the old *harpy*, she came back while I was still trying to get this fat carrot-muncher to move."

"What did you do?" Lottie asked, enthralled.

Sofie shifted her paws, as though she were rather embarrassed. "I pretended to be one of the model dogs," she admitted.

Lottie stared at her, and then giggled. "What, those horrible plastic ones in the shop? The ones modelling the leads and those horrible dog coats?"

"I sat in one of the baskets for sale." Sofie nodded. "I am unnaturally perfect, after all. She thought I was plastic." She twisted her neck and shuddered. "But I had to stay still for a very long time. My neck is still stiff." Then she frowned at Barney. "Who knows how long I would have had to be there, but then, Lottie, you told this idiot to come."

Barney nodded. "You spoke to me," he agreed proudly. "I spoke back."

Sofie rolled her eyes. "*Sacré bleu,*" she muttered.

"So . . . when I called, Sofie was already there?" Lottie worked out.

"Of course." Sofie nodded. "And when the old woman went out to make tea, I opened his cage – the simplest catch you can imagine, why he had not done it himself, I do not know – and I made him follow me here."

"Didn't anyone notice you?" Uncle Jack asked faintly. "A dog and a rabbit, running down the street?"

Sofie wrinkled her nose. "A few people may have done," she admitted. "But it was getting dark." She sighed. "And we did a lot of hiding. Rabbits, as I said, are not brave."

"Afraid not," Barney agreed, his whiskers shivering.

"We'd better find somewhere for you to sleep," Uncle Jack said thoughtfully. "Do you like to sleep in hay? I think we've got some in the storeroom. Or perhaps a cardboard box, with an old towel in it? In one of the bigger cages?"

"A box. . ." Barney agreed blissfully.

Sofie looked expressively at her velvet cushion.

"A box. . ." She shook her head. "Lottie, I am hungry. I have only had a Marmite sandwich since I left. And a very small biscuit. Or two. And a toffee that someone had left in the playhouse. It was furry, Lottie, but I was *starved*. . . And I have had no coffee at all." She held up a paw, and it did seem to be shaking. "I *need* coffee, you see?"

Barney was sitting by the open door of his cage when Lottie and Sofie came down the next morning. He was watching the shop with an air of interested wonder, his nose twitching with happiness. His grey fur had the most wonderful sheen to it – as though he were actually several different shades, depending on which way you looked at him.

"Hello, Barney." Lottie tickled him behind the ears. "Did you sleep well?"

"Oh, yes, thank you." He looked up at her worriedly. "But did you know, my cage is open."

Sofie stared at him. "Of course we know! We are looking at you! Your nose is sticking out of it!"

Barney jumped back apologetically, his whiskers trembling.

"It's OK, Barney. We don't usually lock the cages," Lottie explained. "When the shop's open we try and make sure they look closed, for when people come in, that's all. You can come out of the cage now if you want."

"Out?" Barney murmured, as though he didn't quite understand the concept.

"Rabbits." Sofie shook her head. "He does not have two brain cells to rub together, Lottie. Do not overtax him," she whispered.

Already Fred and Peach, who shared a cage with the other pink mice a couple of shelves above Barney's, were watching him with interest – Fred hanging upside down to spy while Peach held on to his tail. Lottie frowned at them. She had a feeling they were going to try and dive-bomb past his cage, and the poor thing would probably have a heart attack. Fred tried very hard to look innocent, as though he was just exercising perhaps, and Peach hauled up him rather quickly.

Lottie smiled reassuringly at Barney, and she and Sofie went to grab some breakfast. "I don't think rabbits are actually stupid," Lottie said thoughtfully.

"That one is," Sofie stated flatly, sniffing the cereal boxes. "No. They are all cardboard, these things. I want toast."

"He might just be nervous," Lottie argued.

Sofie raised her eyebrows.

"Well, all right, maybe he isn't the brightest bunny ever, but he's very sweet."

Sofie sniffed. "He is a fluffy *imbecile*."

"But you call me that too, all the time," Lottie pointed out. "Not fluffy, obviously."

Sofie smiled at her, showing very white teeth. "I do," she agreed. Lottie wasn't entirely sure what she meant by that, but she suspected she was being insulted. It was nice that things were back to normal.

Lottie bounded out of the shop that morning to meet Ruby. She was desperate to tell her that Sofie was back, and also that her posters had been a vital part of bringing the little dog home, though not in the way they had expected.

She danced on to the bridge, and Ruby noticed her changed mood at once. "Is she back?" she cried. "Did someone find her and bring her back to you?"

Lottie shook her head. "No. She brought herself back. But she saw the posters, and she loved them. I think she might have stayed away longer if she hadn't had proof I was missing her. So thank you!"

School was so different with that wonderful feeling of closeness with her familiar back again – even if all Sofie did that day was sleep, claiming to be worn out by her adventures. Lottie wasn't sure how Sofie had managed to disappear so completely that she couldn't even sense her. She'd tried asking, but Sofie didn't seem to be able to explain. Lottie was just so glad to have her back, she didn't push the question. At some point she'd talk to Ariadne about it, but right now it felt like a missing piece of her had been slotted back in, and she was whole again. Or almost whole.

Every so often Lottie missed her mother badly, and since her dream on Monday night, she hadn't been able to help thinking about her. What with the rabbit to worry about, and then Sofie going missing, her mind had felt as if it were about to burst. Now that she could think more clearly, she could see why her mother had kept coming into her mind.

What was she going to tell her? And how? She couldn't ring her up and say that her father was alive after all. Her mother wouldn't believe her, and even if she did, it would be the most cruel thing to do. Lottie needed to be with her, holding her. But should she even tell her now anyway? What if the dream had been wrong? What if it was just a dream after all?

Lottie nibbled her pen and tried to look as though she was thinking about the story she was meant to be writing. She scribbled another couple of sentences, to distract Mrs Laurence.

There was only one thing for it. She needed to see her mother. Mum had been promising to take her to Paris soon. Maybe they could talk there. Lottie wished she knew how much time they had before her father came – if he was even coming. . .

Ruby had to go out with her mother after school, so Lottie walked home alone, still tangling with the problem of her parents. She felt as though she wasn't old enough for all this – as though these were grown-up questions. How to reintroduce your dead father to your mother wasn't something ten-year-olds usually had to think about. She knew her mum had missed him desperately, but it was seven years that he'd been gone. Did she still love him, even? Lottie sighed.

Be happy, Lottie! Sofie's voice sang in her mind, with such an air of excitement and secrets that Lottie quickened her pace at once.

Sofie? What have you been doing? What's going on? Come home and see! Sofie told her gleefully.

Arrivals, Sofie's mind seemed to be saying, and Lottie gulped. Was her father here already? Had her dream come true so soon? Lottie broke into a run, her heart thumping. She was excited and terrified at the same time.

She flung open the door of the shop and squeaked with joy. Standing there, cuddling Barney the rabbit, who was lying on his back with his paws in the air looking happier than Lottie had ever seen him, was her mother.

7

Actually, Lottie realized, after she'd delightedly hugged her mother for at least ten minutes, she wasn't just holding a rabbit. She was cuddling an *animal*. Lottie's mum didn't do animals. She'd always resisted Lottie's pleas for a pet by pointing out that she was at work all day, and Lottie was at school, and then after-school club. The poor creature would be lonely. Lottie had tried to argue for a hamster, as they slept in the daytime anyway, or even a fish, but her mum wasn't budging.

So why was she now crooning sweet nothings to Barney while she tickled his tummy like an expert rabbit-handler?

Sofie frowned at her. *I like your mother, Lottie, even though she is strange. But it is very boring not being able to talk while she is here. And she seems rather too fond of rabbits.*

Lottie gave Sofie an apologetic look. *Why is she strange?* she asked curiously. Lottie had always thought of her mum as incredibly, relentlessly normal. It was why she couldn't hear the animals in the shop – because she simply didn't believe that unusual things could happen to her.

Well, she could hear us if she wanted to, Sofie told her. She didn't sound as though she was arguing. Her voice in Lottie's mind was completely matter-of-fact. She knew she was right – even more so than usual.

You mean she doesn't see what's going on here on purpose? Lottie blinked at Sofie, completely confused. *Why?*

Sofie looked at Lottie's mother, with her head on one side and a smidge of tongue sticking out. It was something she did when she was really concentrating.

Perhaps it is easier that way? she asked thoughtfully. *Or maybe she is scared.*

Scared of what? Lottie bit her bottom lip worriedly.

Of what she might have to be if she could see what is real, Sofie said, very slowly. *I think. But it is hard to tell. It is bad manners to snoop around in someone's mind. And there is a very thick fog in her head. She is not doing any of these things on purpose, Lottie. It is just the way her mind works.*

"Lottie!"

Lottie jumped, and her mum laughed. "You really were away with the fairies. Were you thinking about school?"

"Mmm. . ." Lottie smiled. That was typical of Mum. She considered saying, "Not quite; I was talking to the dog," but it didn't seem the right time.

"Your uncle Jack says I can have the room next to yours again, Lottie," Mum explained. "Want to come and help me unpack? I brought you a couple of things," she added persuasively.

Chocolate? Sofie's ears pricked up a little.

Lottie's mum headed for the stairs, still cradling Barney in one arm, and with her holdall in the other.

"Mum? Are you taking Barney upstairs?" Lottie couldn't help asking.

Her mother looked down and laughed, sounding a little embarrassed. "Oh, I forgot I was holding him. He's so cuddly, isn't he? He reminds me of Alfie, the rabbit I had when I was your age, Lottie.

He was a darling, just like this lovely bunny." She looked thoughtful. "Is Barney house-trained, Jack? *Could* we take him upstairs?"

Uncle Jack looked amused, and Barney blinked at him hopefully.

I think I am, he murmured vaguely in their heads.

"I'm sure he'll be fine." Uncle Jack raised his eyebrows at Lottie, who made an *I have no idea!* face back. Her mum, wanting to take an animal up to her bedroom? Her mum, who was always saying pets were unhygienic? Lottie followed her slowly up the stairs, Sofie padding along behind.

Lottie's mum turned as she heard Sofie's claws on the wooden treads. "Oh, Lottie, I've just thought. You don't think Sofie will chase poor Barney, do you? I know she's only little, but dachshunds can be quite snappy."

Lottie stifled a laugh at Sofie's outraged face. Her whiskers were vibrating with horror. "She really won't," she promised her mum, and then she crossed all her fingers behind her back, telegraphed a heartfelt mental apology to Sofie, and told her mum, "Sofie's very well trained."

Sofie held back a growl, letting out just the faintest breath of it, to show Lottie how insulted she was.

She doesn't mean to be rude, Lottie pleaded.

I would like to sweep away that fog from her mind, just so that I can tell her exactly how rude she is being! Sofie snarled. *Snappy! What does she think I am, a Yorkshire terrier?*

Lottie loyally didn't remind Sofie about the various times she'd bitten people, and that she and Uncle Jack had to have a strict no-biting agreement. She was fairly sure Sofie only bit people when it was absolutely necessary. Even if Sofie's views on the subject weren't necessarily the same as everyone else's.

In Lottie's mum's room, Sofie sat disapprovingly on the armchair and watched while Barney pottered around investigating. Lottie's mum unpacked her bag, bringing out a beautiful sweater for Lottie.

No chocolate? Sofie asked wistfully, leaning forward on the armchair to sniff the bag. *Though that is a very chic sweater, Lottie.*

"Lots of girls in Paris seem to be wearing jumpers like that," her mum was saying. "Oh, I have missed you, Lottie. I see all the children going to school in the mornings, and it makes me think of you so much."

Lottie leaned up against her. "Me too. I mean, I miss you too." She hesitated, hopefully. "Are you –

are you staying for long?" Really, she wanted to ask if her mum was coming back soon, but she didn't want to hear her say no.

Her mum frowned. "I'd like to, Lottie, I really would, but I have to go back on Sunday night." She hugged Lottie tightly. "I'm sorry."

"It's OK," Lottie lied. "I can't believe you just turned up. Did you tell Uncle Jack you were coming?"

Her mum smiled. "Yesterday. But I wanted it to be a surprise for you. Did you like it?"

"I love it," Lottie told her, and for once, she didn't feel like she was bending the truth, or trying not to hurt someone's feelings, or holding anything back.

At dinner, Lottie's mum managed not to look disapproving about Sofie eating at the table. Actually, she let Barney sit on her lap, and fed him bits of her salad, while everyone else pretended not to notice.

"So, Isobel, I didn't know you liked rabbits?" Uncle Jack asked, watching a small pink nose appear hopefully at the edge of Lottie's mum's plate, in search of tomatoes.

"I had a rabbit called Alfie when I was younger,"

Lottie's mum explained. "I was telling Lottie. He had a cage for when I was out at school, but most of the time he just wandered round the house. He was great company."

"*You* had a free-range rabbit?" Lottie asked, pasta dripping off her fork as she gazed at her mother in amazement.

Her mum looked a little shamefaced. "He was very tidy," she assured Lottie.

"But you always said pets were no good indoors! You wouldn't let me have a hamster because you said they smell!" Lottie lowered her voice here, in case Giles was listening. His sense of tact was not strong, and Lottie didn't think that even her firmly disbelieving mother could manage to not hear Giles if he started giving her a lecture on good manners and hamster hygiene. Particularly if she used his parade-ground voice.

"I know." Her mum sighed sadly. "I was probably wrong, Lottie. I'm sorry. Seeing you here, with all these lovely animals, I realize it wasn't fair not to let you have a pet. We'll have to think about it carefully when we're back in the flat."

Lottie glanced at her. *When*, not *if*.

Sofie was staring at Lottie with huge, troubled black eyes.

Don't worry, Lottie told her. *I'm not leaving you behind. Whatever she says. And I shouldn't think it'll be for ages, anyway. Mum hasn't mentioned the Paris job finishing.*

Sofie gave the tiniest nod, looking worriedly at Lottie's mum. She didn't finish her pasta.

"Dad, I meant to ask," Danny put in. "What were you doing in Broadford at lunch time? Was it a delivery? I waved, but you didn't see me."

Broadford was the next town, a bit bigger than Netherbridge, and the secondary school was there.

Uncle Jack blinked. "Broadford? No, I was here all day. I knew Isobel was coming and she'd need me to pick her up at the station here."

Danny looked confused. He looked over his shoulder at Septimus, who was sitting in his hood again (Lottie's mum hadn't noticed this, thankfully. Lottie was sure she'd be a bit funny about rats). Lottie saw Septimus nod. "It looked exactly like you, Dad. . ." Danny went on. He grinned suddenly. "Were you buying my birthday present?"

From Uncle Jack's sudden expression of panic, Lottie was convinced he'd forgotten Danny's birthday entirely. He even made a discreet note on the back of his hand in biro.

Danny was looking anxious now. "Did you see that magazine I left out for you to find?" he asked. "I circled the games I wanted. You did get the right ones, didn't you, Dad? I don't want another one about pink and purple ponies, *please*. . ."

"I thought that game looked rather nice," his father muttered huffily. "I will find the magazine, Daniel. But it wasn't me in Broadford. Ask your aunt. I was picking her up at lunch time."

Lottie's mum nodded. "He really was, Danny."

Danny frowned. "Wow. I could have sworn it was you, Dad. Although you did have a funny yellow coat on. Weird."

The back door clicked open, and Ariadne came in frowning. She did a double take when she saw Uncle Jack, her frown deepening. "Jack, the strangest thing – oh, hello Isobel, how nice to see you! – Jack, I've just seen you – or someone so like you I would have sworn it was you – walking down the road to Netherbridge Hill. I called after you, but you just didn't seem to hear. And then you slipped out of sight, and there was a. . ." She tailed off, raising her hand to her mouth and biting on her fingertips nervously, as though she'd meant to say something and thought better of it.

Lottie watched her, her heart racing so hard she

felt dizzy. She was almost sure that Ariadne wanted to say that there had been a unicorn.

Lottie and her mum took Sofie for a walk the next morning. Ruby was coming for lunch at the shop later, which felt strange, because Lottie knew her so well now that it seemed as though Mum ought to have met her before.

"Have we got time to go and get a coffee and some cake at that nice café?" Mum asked. "I know it's chilly, but we could sit outside with Sofie, couldn't we?" She reached down to stroke Sofie's head. "She can have an *espresso*. That's her favourite, isn't it?"

Sofie stopped dead and stared up at her in amazement, and Lottie's mum stared back. "Goodness, she really is a caffeine addict, Lottie. She definitely understood what I just said."

"She understands a lot," Lottie told her, trying not to laugh.

They sat outside, wriggling on the chilly metal chairs as they waited for the drinks to come. Sofie sat on Lottie's lap, but she graciously allowed Lottie's mum to stroke her ears.

"She seems different, Lottie," Sofie whispered, when Lottie's mother had nipped to the loo.

"I know," Lottie murmured back. "I think it's Barney. She must have really loved that rabbit she had when she was little, Sofie, and Barney's brought it all back to her. I couldn't believe her feeding him lettuce under the table last night – she was like – well, she was like me!" Lottie looked hopefully at Sofie. "Do you think maybe she's starting to open up a bit? I might be able to tell her about you. . ." She stroked Sofie's head lovingly.

"It is a good thing that rabbits don't like chocolate," Sofie said, with a slightly anxious look. "Or it might be difficult."

"Can you imagine Barney drinking coffee?" Lottie giggled. They were laughing about this when Lottie looked up and saw her mother standing in the doorway of the café, gripping on to the door frame as though she was frightened everything might fall apart if she let go.

Lottie half stood up, clutching Sofie to her, and then she realized that her mother was staring at something in the distance. Lottie turned to see, and gasped.

Just turning the corner of the road was someone that Lottie would have been prepared to swear was Uncle Jack. Except that she knew Uncle Jack was making flea treatment that morning, because he'd banned everyone from the workroom. And so that man had to be her father.

"Get her, Lottie," Sofie snapped – there was no one to hear but Lottie's mum, and she was in a world of her own. "Before she falls."

Lottie sprang up to lead her mum back to her chair, pushing her into it, even though her mum's legs didn't seem to want to bend. Lottie kept hold of her hand, and Sofie jumped from the spare chair on to Lottie's mum's lap. She looked down, vaguely surprised, but she laid her other hand on the little dog's back and mechanically stroked it. Lottie watched, pleased. She knew how comforting Sofie could be when she put her mind to it.

"What happened?" she asked gently. She knew what had happened, of course, but her mum didn't realize that.

"Your father," her mum murmured. "I thought I just saw your father, walking down the road. He didn't see me. He walked away from me." The coffee had arrived while her mum was gone, so Lottie guided her cup to her mouth. Anything to distract her, to bring her out of this fixed trance. Her mum sipped quietly, and the faraway look slipped out of her eyes. She was still white, but she was herself again.

"I'm sorry, Lottie. It was just such a shock. Of course, it wasn't really your father, but it looked so like him. And here, of all places. Did you see him?"

Lottie shook her head. "Only the back of someone." Although even then it had been clear who it was. What should she say? Lottie just didn't feel brave enough to break the news. Not when the merest glimpse of someone her mother didn't even think was him could do this to her. How could she tell her that he was really alive – that he'd been living away from her all this time? "It looked a bit like Uncle Jack."

Her mother took a deep drink of her coffee, shivering slightly. "Being here, Lottie, it brings it all back. And you're so like him. You look like him, of course, more every year, but you're like him in other ways too. Seeing you here at the shop – he loved living there too, you know. He and Jack were so close, and then there were the animals, he was so good with them, any sort of creature. You're the same." She smiled sadly. "I just couldn't carry on here, after he went. Everyone missed him, not only me. You kept asking where he was, and when he was coming home. Every day I had to see Jack, who was so like him.

Sometimes I'd walk into a room and see Jack, and think it was Tom, and I'd be so happy, so grateful that he was back. And then it would hit me that it wasn't. It was as though he died a little more every time." She sipped the coffee again, gazing down the street where Lottie's dad had disappeared. "I'm sorry, it must have been really frightening when I reacted like that just now. But it was like losing him all over again."

"I thought you were going to faint," Lottie told her.

Her mum smiled. "I thought I was too."

"You still miss him, don't you?" Lottie asked, tentatively. "It's been a long time."

Her mum sighed. "Well, it hasn't changed since he went. I mean, it's like a cut's hardened over, but it's still there hurting. I don't think I'll ever stop missing him." She smiled at Lottie. "This is our place for serious talks, isn't it? When we were here last time, you wanted to know all about your dad, and why I wouldn't talk about him. Lottie, I can be furious with him for going off on that stupid trip and still love him to bits at the same time, you know." She sighed. "It's actually quite nice to talk about him. I should have told you about him properly before."

"Are you – are you sure he's dead?" Lottie asked suddenly. She was testing the water.

"Oh, Lottie," her mum sighed. "Have you been hoping all this time? I'm sorry, Lottie love, but he has to be. It's been so long. I wondered, for the first year or so – it made me even angrier, not knowing. . . He wouldn't have just left us, Lottie. I know I said he wasn't a sensible sort of person, but he wouldn't do that." She stroked Lottie's hair. "He loved you so much, Lottie. He'd never have abandoned you."

But he did, Lottie wanted to scream. She'd been wondering about this ever since she'd realized who the unicorn who'd saved her from Pandora really was. Why had he stayed away so long? How could he leave her mother with grief that was like an unhealed wound, and his little girl Lottie without a father?

8

Lottie was sure that she saw her father again on Sunday, just as her mum was gathering her things together to go to the station. A tall, dark-haired man looked into the shop window, just for a second, and then passed on. Lottie froze, staring after him, but no one else had noticed. He seemed to be getting closer and closer, Lottie thought, digging her fingernails into her palms. It was an odd feeling, to want something so badly and be so terrified at the same time. What was he waiting for? Was he going to turn up before her mother left, or not? Lottie wasn't even sure which to hope for.

Uncle Jack was going to drop Lottie and her mum at the station, leaving them to say goodbye, and then Lottie would walk back. It wasn't all that far, and she'd have Sofie for company. Her mum had been doubtful, but Lottie promised her that Sofie was very good protection, and Sofie had demonstrated all her teeth in a wolfish smile. Lottie was sure her mum didn't realize how much she went about alone in Netherbridge. She would be horrified if she knew about everything Lottie had been doing over the last few months.

They walked into the station together, and her mum sighed. "Oh, look, the train's late." She glanced around for a seat. "Let's sit over here, Lottie. I'm glad, actually; I want to talk to you."

Lottie blinked worriedly. They'd talked a lot this weekend, hadn't they? What more did her mum need to say, without anyone else around?

I do not like the sound of this, Sofie muttered in her mind.

Me neither. Lottie rubbed her comfortingly behind her ears, but the muscles were tense under Sofie's soft black fur.

Lottie's mum fussed with her bag for a moment, then looked up, very firmly letting go of the zip she'd been fiddling with. "Lottie, I've been thinking this weekend. I really hate being so far away from you." She reached for the zip again, but stopped herself. "I went to Paris because I was worried about losing my job, and I hated the idea of not having enough money to look after you properly. I never wanted you to miss out because you'd lost your dad – I mean, how could I let you lose out twice over? But what you said yesterday, about whether I was sure he was really dead. . . And I've never talked to you about him properly." Lottie's mum took a deep breath. "I think we need to spend more time together, Lottie. I'm going to tell work that I have to move back here from Paris. If they don't like it and I lose my job, then that's just going to have to be the way it is. I know I can find something else, but it might not be as well paid, that's all. We might have to go without a few things." She looked at Lottie, and Lottie realized with horror that her mum was scared. She was frightened Lottie was going to throw a strop about no more iPods and pretty French sweaters.

"That doesn't matter," Lottie stammered. The awful thing was, a few months ago, she would have been delighted about this. She'd been begging her mum not to go to Paris and abandon her. Lottie hadn't spoken to her for two days before she went, because she was so angry. Now she'd got exactly what she wanted – a mum who finally understood that Lottie cared more about time with her than she did about having money for *stuff*. It was just that she didn't want that any more. Or rather, she did, but she wanted a dad as well. And a dog. And a shop full of talking animals.

How exactly did she explain that one?

Lottie.

Lottie flinched from Sofie's voice in her mind. She didn't know what to say to her right now. She'd promised Sofie that if this happened, she wouldn't let her mum take her away from the shop, and more importantly from Sofie. But what was she going to say? Her mum would be incredibly hurt if she said she'd rather stay with Uncle Jack and Danny, especially when she'd just made such a hard decision. Lottie couldn't tell her about the shop, and even though Mum knew she loved Sofie, she had no idea what their relationship really was. Lottie couldn't explain that Sofie actually knew her better than her mum would ever be able to.

I'll work something out, I promise, she told Sofie, trying to sound reassuring.

LOTTIE!

What?

Sofie sounded exasperated. *That rabbit is here! Look!*

Lottie's mum's fiddling with the zip on her bag had left it half open, and a creamy-pink nose was whiffling cautiously out of the gap. Barney got one soft grey ear and one dark eye above the zip and gave Lottie an apologetic sideways look.

Lottie giggled, glad to break the tension. "Mum. . ."

"What is it?" her mum asked anxiously.

"Barney's in your bag. You know, if you try to smuggle him on to the Eurostar, you could be in big trouble. . ." Lottie put on a mock scolding face.

Her mum's worried expression dissolved. "Oh, Barney. . . What are you doing here?"

Barney scrambled out of the bag completely and snuggled into her lap with the most ridiculous expression of rabbity smugness.

"Poor baby, I can't take you with me," Lottie's mum murmured. "Well, not right now, anyway. I wonder if we could have a rabbit in the flat – he's so good. . ."

The loudspeaker crackled and announced that the train was now arriving, and Lottie's mum looked flustered. "Can you manage taking Barney back to the shop as well as Sofie?" she asked. "I could call Jack and get him to pick you up."

Lottie shook her head. "It's fine. Look, Barney can fit in my bag."

But I wanted her to take me! Barney protested, as Lottie tried to squidge him into her shoulder bag. *She's so nice!*

Lottie sighed mentally. *I'm nice too, and she's coming back, Barney. But she has to go on a train now. You wouldn't like it.*

Wouldn't I?

No, Sofie told him, her voice hard. She was very upset. *Big, loud and scary.*

Oh. But she's coming back.

Yes, Lottie promised.

Good.

"Lottie, I'll let you know what's going on, all right? I probably won't be able to come back at once; I'm on a month's notice in the Paris job, and they might need me to stay for all of that, I'm not sure. But it won't be that long." She smiled lovingly at Lottie. "Things will go back to the way they were, I promise."

Lottie waved her off, one arm round Sofie, who was wriggling with fury, and the other stopping Barney climbing out of her bag.

She knew things could never go back. She didn't want them to, either.

It was a cold, grey Sunday afternoon, thankfully. It meant that hardly anyone saw Lottie struggling home with a furious dachshund and an overemotional rabbit.

"You did not tell her," Sofie muttered, as she pattered down the street from the station. It had started to drizzle and Lottie felt like crying. "A month! I knew you would not say. In a month's time you will be gone, and I will be all alone."

"No, I won't," Lottie told her firmly.

"But you did not tell her that!" Sofie growled.

"I can't do it all at once, Sofie. She's coming back to England because of me. What am I supposed to say, 'Sorry, I don't actually want to live with you any more'? Think about it!"

"So what are you going to do?" Sofie demanded.

Lottie shrugged. "I can't plan anything, Sofie. If that *is* my dad we keep seeing, or even if it isn't, when he actually turns up everything's going to change again, isn't it?"

"Oh!" Sofie stopped and looked up at her. "You mean, we might live with him?"

Lottie shut her eyes, hoping she wasn't tempting fate. "Mum still loves him. Why shouldn't they live together like they used to?" She opened them again, and the sky didn't seem to have fallen in, so she went on. "They used to have the big room underneath mine. Mum told me. It's really nice." She took a deep breath. "And if they did come back here, I think I'd tell her about you all. It isn't fair that she doesn't know. I couldn't imagine telling her before this weekend, but seeing her with Barney, it made me look at her so differently. I could make her believe, I know I could."

"Would she want to?" Sofie asked quietly. "Your father never told her. He must have had reason not to."

"That was because of Pandora! And Mum wasn't happy here before," Lottie argued. "I'm sure it's because she knew inside that everyone was hiding stuff from her."

"That isn't nice," Barney put in sadly.

Lottie jumped; she hadn't realized he was listening.

"Your mother will think you are just making it all up. Then she will drag you away from me because she will think you have gone mad," Sofie said gloomily.

"We'll make her understand. I know she can. How could my dad have fallen in love with her if she was completely blind to magic? How could she have had me?" Lottie argued.

"Your father fell in love with her because she was the opposite of Pandora. He *wanted* somebody without magic," Sofie reminded her. "And you inherited *his* talent; it was nothing to do with your mother."

"Sofie, are you determined to be miserable?" Lottie asked crossly.

"I am only being realistic," Sofie muttered.

"OK, look. Put it this way. If my dad doesn't turn up, or even if he does and she doesn't believe us, and she still wants to move back to our old flat, I will refuse to leave the shop without you. We'll just have to find somewhere to live where you can come too. She can't make me leave you behind! Come on, Sofie, if I have to, I'll put a spell on her!"

"You do not know enough," Sofie whispered, looking away.

"Uncle Jack would help, and so would Ariadne. They know we can't be split up. Sofie, please. You have to believe I won't leave you behind." Lottie crouched down beside her. "Is this still about you thinking I didn't want you any more? I thought you understood."

"I do." Sofie looked up at her. "Most of me does. A few bits of me are not sure. That is all," she added with dignity, and she walked on, holding her head very high. "Come along, Lottie. It is cold."

Back at the shop, Lottie went to find some carrots to cheer Barney up. He was missing her mum already. She thought Sofie deserved something nice too, so she made her some proper coffee in the cafetière, with twice the amount of coffee that it said on the packet.

Uncle Jack had gone to see someone about greenfinches that could turn into bluebirds, apparently, and Danny was "doing his homework", i.e., playing on the computer. It was pleasantly quiet. Lottie went back through to the shop and sat by the counter with her chin in her hands. Sofie sat on the counter with her and stared at her through the steam from her bowl of coffee. It made her look like something from an old film – the kind of thing Lottie's mum liked to watch on Sunday afternoons sometimes, with people saying emotional goodbyes next to steam trains. *I'm not saying goodbye to Sofie*, Lottie told herself firmly. *Whatever Mum says, I will make it work. I will make us all a family somehow.*

She blinked. She hadn't realized so clearly before that this was what she wanted. She had a perfectly good family – she and Mum had been fine together until the Paris move. And she loved living with Uncle Jack and his mad animal family.

But now something inside her seemed to be telling Lottie that wasn't enough any more. All of a sudden she wanted Mummy, Daddy, Lottie and their pet dog. Like something from a storybook.

Storybooks aren't real, Lottie's sensible self said. *That's why they're stories. No one has a perfect family like that. Not really. Even if it looks that way.*

Fred the pink mouse popped his head over the countertop. "Are you having snacks?" he asked hopefully. "Got any raisins? I'm starved, the others are all asleep." He was holding his tail in one little pink paw and twirling it eagerly.

Lottie sighed and fetched the bag of raisins from the kitchen cupboard, pouring out a small pile for Fred. The raisins were the size of buns in his tiny paws, and he nibbled blissfully.

The shop bell rang as the door clicked open, and her uncle's tall figure shambled in.

"You're back early. There's some coffee left if you want some," Lottie told him, picking up a raisin that had slipped from Fred's grasp. Then she realized that Sofie was gazing round-eyed at the figure in the doorway, and she looked up too.

"That would be nice," her father said politely.

Lottie stared wordlessly, and the strange, familiar figure stared back. He was very like Uncle Jack. So alike that if you didn't look straight at him, you could mix them up. But when she looked properly, it was obvious. How could she not have seen? He had the same yellow oilskin jacket on that he'd been wearing in her dream – the funny coat that Danny had seen.

Lottie had to swallow before she could speak. "Where have you been?" she asked at last. It was all she could think of to say.

Her father blinked, his expression troubled. "I've been – I've been away. . ." He shook slightly, and swallowed, as though he was frightened.

"She has missed you," Sofie told Lottie's dad accusingly. "They all have. You should not have been gone so long."

He looked at Lottie, his eyes bewildered, as

though he wasn't sure what he was being accused of. "I'm sorry," he murmured.

"Where were you?" Lottie asked again. "Uncle Jack said you went to the rainforests, to look for unicorns."

Her father's eyes clouded with some great effort as he heard the name. "Jack. Yes. Yes, I found the unicorns. I'm sure I did."

Lottie and Sofie exchanged worried glances, and Fred skittered across the table, looking up at him. Lottie's dad smiled wearily at the little pink mouse and whispered, "Nice colour."

"Thank you." Fred beamed, and ran up his arm to stand on his shoulder. "I like being high up. You're big, aren't you? Is this a friend of yours, Lottie?"

Like most of the mice, Fred had a butterfly brain. Lottie had told him about her strange dreams of unicorns, she was sure, but he hadn't made the connection. He had no idea who this pleasantly tall person was.

Lottie nodded. "I suppose so," she said quietly, looking into her father's eyes, hoping for him to smile, and scoop her up in his arms, and hug her.

He didn't. He coughed, nervously, and tried to smile.

With dawning horror, Lottie knew as he spoke what he was about to say.

"I'm sorry, I'm sure I should know, but – who are you?"

Lottie swallowed. She didn't know how to answer him. She blinked back the tears of disappointment – this was not how she'd pictured her father coming home, not at all. Trying to smile, she told him in a thin little voice, "I'm Lottie." She couldn't bear to add, "Your daughter." It was too hard to have to tell him. He should know! "Would you like that coffee, then?" she added, turning away from him and half-running back into the kitchen, to have a moment to hide her tears.

Her father followed her, and watched her pouring the coffee.

"Lottie. . ." he said slowly. "I know you. Why do I know you?"

Lottie put the coffee in front of him and looked up into his eyes – exactly like her own, everyone had always said.

Her father was home, and he wanted to know her story – and his own. Where should she begin? Lottie smiled at him and took a deep, slow breath – forcing herself to keep calm, and not scream out that she was his daughter. It didn't matter, after all, if it took time for him to remember.

All that mattered was that she had a father again.

Have you read Lottie's first adventure?

Catmagic

HOLLY WEBB

1

I am not looking, I am not looking.

Lottie glared straight ahead, ignoring her mother, who was waving determinedly at her through the train window.

Lottie had hardly spoken to her since she'd broken the news two days ago. She was too angry – and if they discussed it, talked it all through, it would be real. Until just about now, Lottie had been convinced that somehow her mum's new job in Paris wasn't really going to happen, that if Lottie really hated the idea, her mum wouldn't go through with it. But it was getting too late to turn back now.

She wasn't going to see her mum all summer and they hadn't even properly said goodbye! Lottie turned suddenly, pressing her hand against the window.

Her mum wasn't there.

The train had already started, and all Lottie could see were strange faces gliding by. She turned right round in her seat, panicking. She didn't even know when she'd see Mum again! Peering frantically out of the corner of the window as the train curved out of the platform, she could see her mum's pink coat. She was still waving. Lottie waved back until the train was right out of the station. Then she sat down again, feeling shaky and sick, and very alone.

A crackly voice over the speaker announced the stations, loads of them, with Netherbridge Halt buried somewhere in the middle. All at once Lottie stopped feeling miserable and went back to being just plain cross. Netherbridge was a tiny little town in the depths of the country somewhere, and Mum was dumping her there. In fact, she wasn't even taking the time to dump Lottie in person, she was just putting her on the train, and leaving her uncle Jack to pick her up at the other end.

"I can't even remember what he looks like," Lottie muttered crossly to herself, blinking back tears. She had met him before, but it was ages ago, at a family party that her mum hadn't really wanted to go to. Lottie's mum didn't like being around Lottie's dad's family any more. She said it made her feel too sad.

Uncle Jack was Lottie's dad's older brother, and he ran a pet shop in Netherbridge. Lottie had never been there, but she'd seen it in the photos Uncle Jack sent every year in his Christmas card. She had one, actually, in her bag. Mum had given it to her, so she would recognize Uncle Jack at the station.

She rummaged through her bag, at last finding the photo wedged inside her book.

Uncle Jack looked very like the photos of Lottie's father. He had the same curly black hair that Lottie had inherited, and very dark eyes. Usually that would have fascinated her, but right now Lottie was less interested in her uncle than the shop behind him – where she was going to be living for the summer. Her mood lifted slightly. Lottie's mum had always been anti-pet, very much so. She said animals were messy and smelly, and wouldn't fit in a flat. Even goldfish, which Lottie didn't think was very reasonable. It would be fun to be around some animals for once – it didn't look like Uncle Jack's was the boring sort of pet shop that only sold collars and cat toys. She peered carefully at the photo. It was hard to see much, but there seemed to be a parrot on a perch in the window, as well as the bags of pet foods. The sign above the shop said Grace's Pet Shop, and there was something else written underneath, but it was too small in the photo to see.

Grace's Pet Shop. It was quite nice to be going somewhere that had her own name written up above the door. Of course, it would have, Uncle Jack being her dad's brother. Lottie leaned back in her seat, staring dreamily out of the window, and wondering what sort of animals the pet shop might have. Kittens, maybe? A small knot of excitement began to grow inside her – not that she was anywhere close to being happy about all this, of course not. She was furious. But there was no point in being so angry she didn't get to enjoy herself at all. It wasn't as if her mum would be around to see whether she was happy or not. Whenever she phoned, Lottie could quite easily be miserable.

Lottie was rather silent in the van on the way back to Uncle Jack's. She'd managed to forget on purpose that Uncle Jack's son, Danny, would be around too – even after Mum kept going on about how nice it would be to get to know her cousin. Danny was only a year older than Lottie was, but he was a lot bigger than her, and extremely good-looking, and he seemed very sure of himself. Not that Lottie was shy, not normally anyway, but it was hard to know what to say to him. Were they supposed to be friends just because they were related? Lottie supposed it was a bit weird for him too, suddenly having a cousin he hardly knew dumped in his house. Danny wasn't unfriendly, but he just gazed out of the window, and didn't talk, which made it even more noticeable that her uncle was trying very hard to keep the conversation going.

Uncle Jack's van smelled weird, Lottie thought, trying not to sniff too obviously. Maybe it was pet food? She jumped suddenly as something cold was pushed against her hand. Uncle Jack heard her gasp and turned round. The van swerved.

"Dad, watch it! You're driving!" Danny yelled.

"Sorry, sorry!" Uncle Jack murmured, waving apologetically at the driver of the car behind who was looking a bit unnerved. "Don't worry, Lottie, it's just Sofie, she was asleep in there, I should have warned you."

Lottie looked down at the pile of blankets she'd thought she was sitting next to. It was wriggling, and now a damp black nose emerged, followed by a pointed muzzle, and a pair of liquid brown eyes. The little dog twitched her ginger eyebrows at Lottie, and lifted the side of her mouth in an unmistakable smile.

Danny looked over his seat, and let out a low whistle. "You're lucky, she likes you."

"How do you know?" Lottie asked, stroking Sofie's nose.

Danny turned back round, grinning. "She hasn't bitten your hand off."

Lottie gave the dog a doubtful look, and then frowned. It almost looked like Sofie had winked at her.

"Now, that's not fair," Uncle Jack disagreed. "All dachshunds are temperamental. Sofie's just choosy about the company she keeps."

"Yeah, tell that to the postman. . ." Danny said, smirking.

"He trod on her!" Uncle Jack said indignantly.

Sofie swarmed her way out of the blankets and coiled herself into Lottie's lap, where she gazed up at her innocently. *Me. . .?* she seemed to be saying. She was a beautiful dog, shiny black, with ginger paws and those amazing ginger eyebrows. She looked as though she'd been polished. She answered one question anyway – it looked as though Lottie would get to spend the holiday with at least one animal.

They parked in a yard behind the pet shop, and went in the back way. Uncle Jack dropped Lottie's bags, and went to turn over the Closed sign on the door, while Lottie looked round in amazement, still hugging Sofie tightly. She'd never imagined anything like this. The shop was in an odd, crooked little house on the high street – Lottie had had a brief glimpse of the front as they drove past. It was black and white, with a big, many-paned bay window that took up the whole of the narrow front. But it seemed somehow to be much larger on the inside, full of corners and alcoves and niches. Every inch was packed with cages and tanks, wedged together all the way up the walls. It was oddly silent, and Lottie had the disconcerting feeling that she was being watched – almost examined. Then she decided she must be imagining things as the shop was filled with the squeak and scuffle of hundreds of tiny creatures.

Uncle Jack turned back from the door, smiling. "Well, here you are, Lottie. Grace's Pet Shop. Otherwise known as the Mouse Emporium!"

2

Lottie sat on her new bed, looking round the bedroom. It was really sweet. It had obviously been a little girl's bedroom sometime before, because it had pink spotty curtains and pale pink walls. The bedclothes had pink spots too. In fact, there was something very weird about those pink spots. Lottie was sure she'd seen them before somewhere. Maybe one of her friends had something similar. Although, to be honest, the whole room felt familiar. She leaned back against the wall, staring round thoughtfully. The room was right at the top of the house, so it had a sloping ceiling, and the window was oddly crooked. No one she knew had a bedroom like this. So why did it feel like she'd been here before?

"Lottie!" Her uncle was yelling up the stairs. "Come and have a drink!"

Lottie gave one last considering look around, shook her head, and went downstairs.

Uncle Jack and Danny were in the shop, sitting on stools by the counter with drinks and biscuits.

"I still think we're never going to get away with it," Danny said, shrugging. "How can we?"

"We just need to be a bit careful, it might not be for long," Uncle Jack told him soothingly, but he looked worried.

"Well, how long is she staying? I don't get it, does her mum just not want her or something—" Then he saw Lottie coming and shut up, shoving a biscuit into his mouth whole instead.

Uncle Jack looked very embarrassed. His ears turned red and he glared at Danny. "Lottie! Tea? Orange juice? Have a biscuit!"

It was obvious they'd been talking about her. Lottie supposed it was only natural, but she couldn't help feeling hurt. Especially because Danny had summed up exactly what she felt. Lottie's mum's exciting career move to Paris was more important than her own daughter. Suddenly she was blinking back tears, and she stared very hard at one of the cages without really looking at what was in it.

"Do you like mice?" Uncle Jack asked hopefully, moving over to her.

"Yes," Lottie sniffed. It wasn't as if she'd ever really known any, but she was sure she did. Blinking again, she realized that the cage she was staring at so hard was full of beautiful little white mice, so tiny and delicate, with ruby-red eyes. They were all looking at her, interestedly. It was quite odd to be stared at by mice.

"A new face," Uncle Jack said, rather hurriedly. "Very curious, mice. Always like to know what's going on. Don't you? Mmmm." He tapped the cage-front affectionately, and the mice skittered off.

Lottie looked round at some of the other cages. "You've got a lot of mice," she said in surprise. Several of the cages held mice, in all different colours. Lottie peered carefully at the topmost cage. Were those mice *pink*?

"Oh, we specialize in mice." Uncle Jack hurriedly steered Lottie to a cageful of beautiful glossy black ones. "We *are* the Mouse Emporium. But we have almost everything else too. Kittens, rats, lizards, goldfinches. We had a scorpion until last week, he was *very* interesting." Uncle Jack looked thoughtful. "He was quite sneaky though, kept getting out of his tank. Bit of a worry."

"Miracle we're still alive," Danny muttered.

Lottie squirmed, feeling suddenly itchy. She hoped none of the other pets were given to escaping. Especially not the small ones, with lots of legs. . .

"Your mum said you liked animals?" Uncle Jack suggested hopefully.

"Oh yes!" Lottie nodded. "Would I be allowed to help in the shop at all?" she asked shyly.

Uncle Jack looked like he wanted to hug her, and

Danny gave a cough that sounded suspiciously like a snigger.

"Of *course* you can." Uncle Jack led her over to a large run, where four black kittens were playing on some tree branches that had been built into a sort of climbing frame. They had loads of toys too. In fact, all the animals in the shop seemed to have toys and lots of things to do. It was also the cleanest pet shop Lottie had ever seen. "Would you mind playing with these?" her uncle asked anxiously. "They need lots of handling, so as to get used to people, and it's one of those jobs that I just don't get time for."

Lottie grinned. She was getting the feeling she was going to enjoy this summer.

Look out for Lottie's other adventures!

HOLLY WEBB

Hamstermagic

A SPELL-BINDING TAIL

HOLLY WEBB is the author of the bestselling
Lost in the Snow and its sequel, *Lost in the
Storm*, as well as the popular Triplets series.
She has always loved cats and now
owns a very spoilt one.